Original title, *De weg n*
Published by Free Musket

THE ROAD TO OIA
AND ONE OF THEM

GEORGE JAY

America Star Books
Frederick, Maryland

Softcover 9781681224084
PUBLISHED BY AMERICA STAR BOOKS, LLLP
www.americastarbooks.com
Frederick, Maryland

THE ROAD TO OIA

After Aisha's departure, Han considered whether or not he should sell his business and home. He had had enough. "I think I should take some time to get up to speed. Then we shall see. He stood in the studio- workshop and looked around, lost. It was where he had worked for years with devotion. He felt as if he was incomplete. "I've had all the time," he wondered. He considered the meaning of it all. Without meaning, what use was living? "Even without sense, life is meaningless," he thought. Words, words, words. Nonsensical sentences. In this state of mind, he was skeptical about anywhere. "Anyway, I have to leave here. This home exudes of Aisha. It will be a torture if I stay here longer." In his mind, he kicked a leg of the desk as if it was the culprit of his imbalance. His work and the environment that had been home for years were against him. He opened the patio door. He needed fresh air. Hands in his pockets, he sauntered by the pool and at the end and sat on a lawn chair. His gaze wandered through the garden. There was a large gazebo at the back he had built ten years ago. On nice summer days, he and his wife drank there during lunch break, or tea, or coffee with the staff. "What am I doing here alone? Why should I stay longer? Why should I repeatedly confront with my past? Is this an exercise in the near future? Aisha..." He felt pressure in his stomach. Every time he turned, he thought of Aisha. Every breath he took reminded him of Aisha. A cloud passed before the sun and blocked the light. He got up and strolled back to the workshop. He shut the garden door and turned the key with a hard click as if this would make him forget a piece of history. "No," he thought, "I have certainly gone." He walked up the stairs, toasted two slices of bread in the kitchen, filled them with slices of salmon from the fridge, and sprinkled some pepper on them. He poured himself a glass of orange juice. Then, he sat down at the kitchen table and began eating modest meal. While he was eating, he stared straight ahead. Thoughts of the past and slowly came back. He decided that he had to get over it in the shortest possible time. He made himself a cup of coffee and again took place at the table. He wrote some measures on a notepad that seemed of interest to him, like selling the business in the near future.

The next day, he called Delta Lloyd to buy out his savings account. He had placed an ad in the four most famous newspapers in which he listed the building which included the shop, photo studio, technical workshop, and the other workshop. There were two floors of living space, a large garden with a pool and a gazebo, and a detached garage. For the next few days, he worked in the usual manner with the store staff.

"Aisha's visiting relatives abroad," he told the girls. Gradually, they began to suspect that something was going on. After ten days, he received the first responses to his listings. "It's as if they had been waiting for it," he thought. Compared to his solid relationships, he felt obliged in foregoing conscientiousness to settle down. In the following days he devoted his attention largely on selecting the most suitable entrepreneur who wanted to take over the building. After due consideration, there were finally two candidates who possessed sufficient expertise and reputation in his opinion. He had the choice between a group of qualified personnel and a family business in Belgium which has long operated in Brussels. Both interested companies were well regarded. Personal contact to Han seemed the best guarantee in maintaining his policy. His individual approach and craftsmanship had produced excellent financial results in previous years. After he considered the matter of choice on all sides, the Flemings enjoyed his favor.

During their first contact, he met a sympathetic man and expert. His young Dutch wife was homesick and spent her days in her breezy birthplace behind the dunes. The man decided that it would be their domicile in the coast where

Han's business was located. Through a notary acquisition in reasonable time, both parties were satisfactorily regulated. The transfer agreement also included a clause which required the seller to interact and assist the new owner for the next three weeks after the date of the acquisition. In this period, the men worked together on the technical workshop. Already, in the first days, Han had little things to teach the new owner. During the evenings, the men met together in the home and talked matter over. They watched TV or sat talking to the fireplace. They held a glass of whiskey and rocked it in their fingertips. The jovial Fleming peppered Han with stories that were somewhat laded with his melancholy. Between them was a volatile relationship, and it happens among men who are in a period of joint work and leisure. The next Saturday morning had the Belgian driving back to Brussels in his Mercedes. He said he'd come back again on Monday with some clothes for the next week and a few minor items before the final move from Brussels. His little family would come to the Netherlands as soon as his brother, who was also a skilled technician, had acted sufficiently in the leadership of the Brussels branch. During the weekends when Han was home alone, his problems weighed on him the hardest. He had no distraction and sought solace in the workshop where he has been busy. In two weeks, it'll all be over. He was comforted during the first weekend, but still. On one of those last Saturday mornings, he asked the Fleming for his departure date and whether or not he should take two boxes of sleeping pills to Brussels.

"Since my wife left, I've suffered from insomnia. Vesparax is the only means that I still want to help out. In this country, without a medical prescription, it won't be given," he reasoned. In this phase, the photo shop was no longer his property. He felt like a bird in a strange nest. He decided to spread his wings once the contractual obligations were terminated. The large gazebo provisionally could not be used by the new owner. He allowed Han to store some furniture and other belongings in this last winter. They agreed that Aisha could decide what to do with it. The rest was to refuse. Also, after the financial part of the transaction, everything seemed to have settled satisfactorily. Han made half of the available funds and joint investments in Aisha's bank account. A week later, he took a small suitcase and a camera beside him to the airport. Near the Departure, he found a free parking space. He called Aisha from a pay phone. Since she had gone to her mother in the capital, they had avoided any contact. He got her directly on the line.

"It's Han. I'm standing at Schiphol. I'm going away for a while. The property's now been sold," he said as neutral as possible, scraping his throat nervously. "Excuse me. Please. You can pick up our belongings. Everything is stored in the shed. The new owner is an amiable Belgian. His name's Flemish. He knows it."

"I saw your ad two months ago. When I saw my bank statement last week, I thought, I'm suddenly rich. Where are you going?"

Han was hardly surprised.

"I parked the sports car in the North Hall," he dodged. "You can pick it up there. I no longer need it. Do you have another set of keys?" Suddenly, he remembered her interest. "Perhaps you can exchange the trolley for the Little Vehicle," he remarked cynically.

"What do you mean?"

"That should be clear to you," he grinned slyly, although he was glad that he heard her voice, "Flirting with that Buddhist there!"

"Oh...uh...nice."

Both were silent for a moment.

"Well Aisha, I salute you," he said, a little embarrassed about his tactlessness. "I wish you well."

"Don't need the car when you come back?"

"For now, I'm not coming back. What will I find here?"

"Where are you going?"

"I don't know. Maybe wander around a little," he said hesitantly.

"Why aren't you telling me?"

"What does it matter to you?" In the silence that followed, it seemed that it was every man for himself trying to gauge the other's thoughts.

"Aisha, I need to hang up. I need to check in," he said with a dose nonchalance. His heart pounded in his throat at the thought of saying his final farewell.

"Bye," she cried.

The latter escaped him. With a resolute gesture, he settled the handset on the hook. He took a deep breath to refuel his energy. He then took his briefcase and dragged his trolley behind him, making his way to the counter. After taking off the plane, he stared out a window and watched the clouds that drifted like his thoughts from the past.

"I have Tony converted to Buddhism," she stammered nervously without introduction. Han was concentrated in the repair of a TV camera. How long has she been standing in the doorway? The echo of her words lingered in his mind. His breath was freezing cold and before him the clear meaning dawned on him. The timbre of her voice betrayed nervousness. He looked up and realized that she serious. Still, he was shocked. He wanted to express himself in a controlled manner. He waited a few seconds before he responded. Without his work to look at, he noted:

"Presumably you mean Tony has repented? At least, if you want to call it that."

From the corner of his eye he saw her nod. He had the impression that the double bottom of his remark escaped her at this time.

"I said it wrong," she said.

He winced in a crease, trying to grin. Didn't she understand? Both of them were waiting for a word from the other. Han explained additionally, which increased his uncertainty. He wondered how he could fix the situation. A glimpse of a smile played around his mouth at this fallacy. These were no TV cameras! The consequence of his decision was to the extent that he was certain. He could not see constantly. It was not her choice of Buddhism that interested him. That was the background which the essence stood seemed eminently. His harbored suspicions became clear. Tony. She let a trial balloon on. It seemed difficult for him to pierce. He shook his head.

"Strange..." he seemed to hesitate, "Incomprehensible! You, who are so skeptical in every form of religion, to suddenly convert to Buddhism?" He gave her an ironic look. It was also a form of self-reproach, he realized. "That's unfair. You don't do anything like that, and certainly not compared to your beloved partner. Relationship reduced to theater, or something like a kind of power struggle between the sexes. Ridiculous. Stale. Malignant. Foreign word evil and nice. Evil nature.

"It isn't a belief..." she begun.

It was a shaky attempt to lead the conversation to the sidelines, he wondered again.

"The Buddha is beyond religion and rejects the notion of a soul. Buddhism is a way of life, a certain pattern of behavior that gives you freedom to believe or disbelieve." She took a deep breath before she continued. He worked quietly and did not look as if it was a passing notice.

"Prudence. That's all there is to life. Don't use narcotics. Don't steal. Share everything. Dane..."

"Does that make it even for your spouse?" he interrupted her verbiage and gave her a penetrating look. "I must say, you've learned your lesson well. There are only a few insignificant side effects, right? As far as I know, there is something in this Buddhism that reeks of marital infidelity. Was it the western surrogate that brewed Buddhism here? If that's the case, may be for that... uhh Buddhist, shall we say, Tony? "

"Dané refers to food," she stammered sheepishly. Now he knows the real fact and name.

She had not expected such a reaction, he noted. What then? Would he meekly accept the facts?

"Spare me the grandeur of your new belief. Am I not clear enough?" He unwittingly said with an echo of indignation in his words. In the brief silence that followed, he tried to control himself. Her statement had shocked him. Or rather, affected him. Something must have happened between her and the pseudo Buddhist. In his mind, he looked at the dark window where an exuberant outburst like an atomic cloud.

He did not think it would come to that. Originally, he had full of confidence in Aisha. The situation was out of hand. He had to admit that to himself. Everything came over him a feeling of uncertainty. Anyway, his feelings for Aisha, despite her disloyalty, were still the same. It made the affair more complicated and very hurtful. The usually confident Aisha leaned against the door frame. In the years that they were together, never a scene of such a magnitude occurred between them. And now, she felt superfluous. What was she doing here? She was overwhelmed by a tangle of emotions with no way out. It seemed as if she has dropped into an unknown land where a native man performed a miraculous call that couldn't be derived of any meaning. All the blood in her head seemed to have been drained. She felt her heart beat faster and she wanted to return to her room. This loss of confidence, which never happened to her before, made her unable to move.

"And what?" Han's laconic voice sounded in the background as he was a child who just got reprimanded.

"I want to go," she uttered with difficulty. She was aware that this made her appear dubious. Of course, she had not meant it that straight.

"Oh. You want to leave? When? Right now?"

She was sick. She got everything together but she could not focus on the situation clearly. She swallowed a few times before the words came out of her dry mouth:

"Now..." her lips trembled.

Han had to agree with her. Compassion and love are like identical twins in a womb but nevertheless, they are born separate. She needed comfort and he felt the need to take her in his arms. Nevertheless, he heard himself saying abstractly:

"I understand. Tomorrow, we'll talk."

Inconvenienced by the situation, he nodded to her aloofly like a rebuked shop assistant who had made a mistake. At the same time, he felt sorry for his cool arrangement. "Did I just allow myself to be treated so blunt? Why now? If only I had her in my arms... The question is whether or not she could accept that."

He heard her stumble on the staircase. In fact, it was as if it was the most natural thing in the world. These types of calls are made daily. Those involved were always new to it. How can you respond to such an attack on your life? From one moment to another, you find yourself staggering and running with the world under your feet. You stumble in the rear and lose the ability to provide a rational response. Your mind's paralyzed. Or was it wounded self-love? The stories you sometimes heard coming from others in a similar situation fail to make an impression. Through your personal commitment, you live in the assumption that your case is exceptional. Chaos strikes in deeds and thoughts. The feeling you've imagined is laced with a dose of self-love. Incidents require a dominant role. Your mind becomes clouded by side issues that are focused on emotions. Such statements are not sincere and the intentions are misunderstood. Finally, you can even go up and about to substantiate immorality with morals. Each one has their own private ethics with the result being a kind of "morality" as an alibi for one's thoughts and actions. In his mind, he looked anxiously at a rolling screw that had fallen to the ground.

"I should have foreseen this development," he reproached himself. "I was under the false assumption that they would never let it come so far. I was too lax."

Eighteen months ago, Aisha had signed a three-year course in art history. Afterward, she spent the evenings at the TV.

"Television is a breeding ground of boredom," she told Han, who was working in the technical workshop through the intercom. He laughed. "How long are you still going to work?" she asked.

"I'll be ready."

"So, it'll either be another half hour to an hour," she said, coming from experience. She went to the couch and read a book. After a short time, her eyes became tired.

"Of course, you stand there all day," Hans had commented afterward, "Go do something relaxing. Go do gymnastics, fitness, aerobics, yoga, aikido, or maybe even tai chi."

"Yoga seems interesting," she decided after some thought.

"Excellent. This will also keep your mind fit and your figure up to date. You can still have a job even after your classes."

They responded to a small announcement in a magazine. She went to her classes twice a week. She drove to the capital and stayed a few hours away. She took it seriously. On other nights, she practiced from a book and meditated in her room. Outside his business preoccupations, Han only contacted her during meals and on Sundays. It did him good. He continues working. He had decided that he would take due time to familiarize with the way of life of yesteryear. That was his goal. A generous bank balance would make them financially independent and he had that accomplished.

Like a punished schoolgirl, Aisha left the workshop to her inner world of rain, helplessness, and tears. Han's attitude had offended her. It made her feel as if there was a yawning gap between them. She opened her bedroom door as if to isolate herself. "How exaggerated," she thought. She needed to isolate herself. Indecisive, she sat at her dressing table. She had promised to call Tony as the result of a conversation with him. She could not afford to make a phone call now. She kept staring at her reflection. She was thirty-six years old and usually, she looked about eight years younger. Her face showed an ivory skin laden with features of fatigue. She felt empty. The eyes hollow staring at her betrayed a dull mood. She reached for her hand and pressed a radio button. "The Winner Takes It All," warbled a female voice. The music failed to distract her. She switched off the machine. Her thoughts turned increasingly to the conversation. Her thoughts whirled about in her head like balloons in the wind. "How can we deal with each other? We're not enemies! In any case, he knows now," she sighed. "What next? What are the consequences," she contemplated. "Is it wise to put everything on the line for a new, more or less uncertain relationship? What do I really like about Tony? Isn't it risky? Han knows what I did to him. Don't I love him anymore? Does he still love me after all this...? Is Tony trustworthy? That remains to be seen. He is young, in his early thirties... Age says so little," she reassured himself. "The recent years with Han were a rut. I want to decide for life before I die. That superficiality and lack of interest are things I can no longer tolerate. They must come to an end, anyway. Han can't talk. But Tony, Tony... His gentleness, patience, the relaxed atmosphere of meditation; the conversations I could talk with him about the Self and the Meaning of Life, the yoga classes, his patience, his interest, he's a haven of peace."

After a busy day with customers and staff, she was usually too tired for supper. Nevertheless, she started on the days after the end of the meal. Doing dishes cheered her. The ride to the capital in anticipation of a few hours of relaxation calmed her. Han disappears to the workshop every night right after eating. At eleven o'clock, he usually eats a cracker and drinks a glass of wine. Then, he goes back to work like he's hooked to it!

In the previous years, they usually went to the theater. They had a subscription for some concerts and operas. Gradually, the experience became watered down. It was as if Han was married to his work.

"What inspires you? You always work!"

"We need money, honey. Lots of money," he said back then, "We need enough money to be free to do and whatever we want and maybe live somewhere in the south of France or in the Italian Riviera. This requires financial independence as we've planned."

"At the expense of our modern entertainment? How much is enough? One million, two million?"

"With the sale of the business, goodwill, inventory, and property, we'll be on our way soon."

"Can't we go for something less? And make it a bit lively here? How long do you want to keep at it? You also need to think of your health."

"Really dear, it's all for the best. Don't bother hesitating." He smiled tenderly. He wanted to take her in his arms. Annoyed, she repelled him. He smiled at her and gave her a long running a kiss on the neck. "You go and play sweetie!" Aisha felt her opinion didn't count. He hardly gave her any attention. "As if I belong to the inventory." She thought to herself.

In the afternoon, Han arrived at the Hellinikon Athens airport. After the luggage hassles, he took a taxi to Saint George Hotel near Lykabettus hill just outside the hustle and bustle of downtown. His room offered a wide view of the capricious dusty roofs. The falling sun basked the Parthenon on the Acropolis in the distance. At the foot of the hill shimmered the pulverized ruins of the Agora. After unpacking his suitcase, he sought the terrace of the Floca restaurant that same evening. He knew, from a previous holiday, that as he ate he could look at passers-by. As the evening thinned and night crept, his mood dropped. He missed Aisha's company. He paid for his drinks and hailed a cab. The driver took him to a well-known nightclub. Han took his place at an empty table near the entrance. A waiter obliged him to order two drinks at a time. Afterward, the only thing he could recall of the events that night was the face of a belly dancer. As she danced to the beat of the music, her feathered breasts swayed in opposite circles as if they were yo-yos.

Apparently, he had drunk too much. How else could he have awoken the next morning in the bed of an unknown lady? He didn't have a clue. A taxi drove him to his hotel. In his room, he took a lukewarm bath. Then, he threw himself on bed and fell asleep. The next day, he wandered the city with his camera and shot familiar photos of worn objects. By the pool on the roof of the hotel, the crippling afternoon heat was barely tolerable. He lazed on a lounge in the shade. He took little interest in the English and German newspapers. He drank cold beer and sweated at the same again. In the afternoon, he rested for an hour in his room. He thought of setting residence here predominantly and took a nap. The evening brought about a little coolness. He dined late in the Plaka, the old Turkish quarter. At about midnight, he lingered on the terrace of the Hotel Omonia. He followed the crowds to the square and drank iced whiskey. Then, he went back to Saint George Hotel. After four days, he went to Athens. He wanted to book a flight to Santorini or Thera, the island's official name. All flights were booked for more than a week. During this period, he sought to amuse himself and left on a bus to Delphi.

In the busy town, the heat struck him at Parnassus. He later found shelter in a hotel that overlooked a lawn. He saw the endearing friendship between a donkey and a horse. The meals he had in outdoor restaurants where mainly with students from across Western Europe and a bunch of stray Japanese students. He listened to their conversations as far as he could follow them and stayed long after dinner with chilled retsina. As inspiration for untalented painters, the sun threw wide range of varying shades over the peaceful mountains. The Delphi valley stretched as the sun scorched the town of Itea on the Gulf of Corinth. Han took the pedestrian and bus tours in the vicinity. He walked the Sacred Way to the temple of Apollo and searched for the gap above the Pythia in vain. In Stadiou, above the ruins of Apollo, he stretched himself on the hot concrete of single seats. Overpowered by the exhausting heat, he soon drifted into sleep. Afterward, back in the center of Delphi, he read a book about the history of the town. On the way to the terrace of the restaurant where he dined, he became fascinated at the small green brown owl that had a spherical shape. He observed its grim head. His hand in the shop to the round onyx bullet entered and paid. Therapon Brother in arms, he baptized the bird.

"That bastard," croaked the onyx owl when it slid along with the little money in his pocket.

"Is that my new name?" Han grinned.

He didn't spend more than a few days in Delphi before boredom struck. Back in Athens, he took up residence at the Cosmopolitan Hotel. On his last night in Athens, he lived in the Herod Atticus Theatre and saw a performance by Maurice Bejarts Ballet du XXe siècle. The first ballet did not appeal to him. Maria Casares recited as the dancers dragged her across the stage and Bejart writhed on the ground like an earthworm. A second ballet, inspired by India, suited him better. Afterward, he was accosted by a young Greek officer outside the theater:

"Do you like boys, sir? I'll fuck you for two hundred drachmas."

Han strolled back to the hotel, his mind caught up in the past. He could not free himself of it.

Aisha and Roy, her ex-boyfriend, formed an amateur dance couple. In the near future, they wanted to leap to the professional stage. They asked Han shortly before he opened his studio and technical workshop to take some shots of their dance poses for a friendly price. He found them to be a sympathetic couple and shot beautiful shots of the superficial friends for free. About half a year later, he divorced her. Han heard nothing more Roy after that.

His business continued to expand after a year or two. He got busy, with the help of a mortgage, was able to take over the premises. On a Sunday afternoon that late September, he walked in the Haarlem Wood when he met Aisha by chance. She was shuffling through some dry leaves, enjoying the beautiful fall weather.

"All those colors," she said, "makes you marvel at the transition of nature that's so characteristic of autumn."

On a terrace, they drank tea and soda. Then, they walked together for a few hours. Han invited her to go somewhere in Haarlem to eat. Afterward, he took her in his car to the capital where she lived with her mother.

"May I call you again?" he said as they parted.

On the way to his studio on the coast, he mused. Aisha's name fit her graceful appearance excellently. He thought he recognized Hindu influences.

"Nice girl," he muttered, "Aisha."

During the winter months, an intimate relationship flourished between them. In the spring, they went to Sorrento in Italy on holiday. Six months later, they got married. Their marriage lasted almost without dissonances. They had some trivial bickering here and there. Han, during that period, built a reputation for being an excellent photography and film producer. Professionals from almost all the provinces, and even from abroad, sought his services. He did an excellent job at an acceptable price and treated his customers properly. In the last years of this period, making money imperceptibly becomes an obsession for him. Eventually, even his time on weekends were dedicated to work. His mind wandered regularly to the work that awaited him.

In about nine months, he would be fifty years old. A large sum of money was paid to his savings account. His plan was to sell the case along with the property and invest the money in bonds. The interest would provide him ample resources to invest in a mild climate country somewhere south of Europe and enjoy a carefree life. But now, his life was in chaos. He sighed with frustration.

In the port of Piraeus, he booked the boat to Hydra, an island south of Athens. He had spent a week there during his honeymoon. He leaned on the railing of the ship. His gaze slid over the smooth surface of the water while his mind was like a tidal wave that washed over the beach of the past.

"Look at that flat water. There are waves everywhere," laughed a radiant Aisha. She enjoyed the trip, the beautiful weather, and their union. In her brief marriage to Roy, she had felt a loss. After the divorce, things became really clear for her. Roy, with his artistic inclinations as a painter and fickle nature, was never able to provide what she truly needed. She didn't want to change homes every now and then. She needed a place where she could settle. Han, she had found, had no regular tensions and can endure a relationship. In the relatively short time that she dealt with him, she thought it was time to settle down with him.

The boat was hardly rocked by the wind. The sea began to sway and the floor dance like a drunkard. Turkey has been plagued by a minor earthquake and as an offshoot, touched the seabed. Beyond the island of Poros, the ferry suffered from a faulty rudder. The ship was attacked by the unexpectedly high waves and rolled around in an erratic rhythm of wind and waves. It took them a half hour before the crew of the boat succeeded in towing the rudderless ferry. Meanwhile, many passengers had emptied their stomach over the railing. Aisha also became seasick. With an empty stomach and an empty gaze, she sat down in the passenger compartment and stared into space. Finally, after nearly five hours on the high seas, the boat harbored in Hydra. Usually, the crossing took less than three hours. The docked at the quay. Before anyone could go ashore, three or four men aboard. One came at Han.

"Hotel Lotus, Sir?"

"Please," Han pointed to the luggage.

The man took Aisha and Han's luggage in his hand and hurried out.

"Is a little baby again," Han turned anxiously to Aisha before he entered the gangway.

Despite the strong wind, it was warm and sunny on the island. In the family hotel, the guests were received by the elderly owner and they were sent to their room. He apologized:

"Dinner is always in the garden, but it's winter now."

The dining room had the charm of a cultivated cave. Aisha still experienced some discomfort from her seasickness. She did not know whether or not she'd be able to ingest food. Attracted by the romantic surroundings however filled her with life again. During their stay, they ate lunch at Hydra in a beach that was two / three kilometer's walk away. The beach was covered in small boats and a shuttle service was maintained between the port and the hotel. At the convenience of the boat operators, the road for pedestrians had small chunks of red lava rock and that almost made the path impassable.

On one of those sunny afternoons, Aisha and Han fell on the rocks. They got rid of their clothes and left everything in a cavity behind. Then, they dived into the sea. The water enveloped them like a cool cloth. After this blessing, Han climbed short time later at the rock to country. He was injured by the sea urchins that tangled against the rocks underwater. Han's knees were like pin cushions that were covered with black spines. He gently pried them out one by one. With some difficulty, he managed to lift Aisha unscathed from the water. He dried her off with a rough towel and she put on her sexy dress. A boat that overloaded with passers-by was further away from the beach. Han was only wearing a towel. The towel slipped off his hips. From the crowded boat rose jeers and applause. He laughed and waved a naked salute. Refreshed by the swim, he rested on the warm mossy cavity. He cherished the late afternoon sun. Han, overwhelmed by the situation and Aisha's beauty, realized his wealth. Aisha, since their union, had flourished into a beauty and was emanating a youthful aura of a young girl. As she freshened up in the late sunlight, he crept towards her. "An eternal moment." Those were his words, if he remembered correctly.

"In search of lost love," Han sighed scornfully. "He is never born; he lives in eternal paradise."

Rock Hydra opened and the boat was sent to the bay. It was a natural haven for goods, water, and tourists. It was a stopping place for yachts and cruise ships. In the recent years, little has changed. The islet was still free of cars. During the daytime, Han was on the beach of the big hotel. He sat on a terrace that overlooked the quay. He ordered a modest lunch, drank espresso with Cointreau, and looked at the activity of the new guests. He spent his evenings in some nightclubs located high on the rock. From here, they had to face the harbor bars downstairs where the men put their arms around each other's shoulders and he hopped on the whimper of the Sirtaki.

Hydra once served as home to artists who sought peace to work. This period has long since passed. Now, the island was annexed by recreationists and hordes of day trippers. Han was attacked by a relentless stream of memories. He became melancholic about it. "I should not take this nostalgic trip," he concluded.

To pass the time, he took a day trip to Spetzai. After a stay of three days, he sailed back to Athens.

After "Tony," as Han called him, won the SIOS diploma, he was appointed as a physical education teacher at a secondary school. Shortly afterward, he married his childhood friend Gerda. Initially, in their first years of marriage, nurse for the evening and night shifts in a retirement home. When they finally moved to a house and had furnished it completely, she promised to change jobs. In the subsequent period, they were together every night at home. When that wore off, boredom hit. To give their marriage relationship a boost, they decided to have a child. The child, in all respects, only caused parental frustration. After more than a year, a second child came. Tony felt himself slipping into the sluggish environment. Gerda, who instinctively went in the cult of motherhood, was worried about him. Together with a colleague, Tony bought a catamaran which they wanted to take part in sailing competitions. Gerda was in full term and let her friend join him. He could sail as often as he wanted without making any objections. She stayed at home or went with the children to her parents' weekends. Despite his large dose of freedom, Tony was moody especially in the winter months, when he could not go boating in his free time. At home, he hung jaded on the bench in front of the TV, turning from one channel to another. Meanwhile, he stuffed his face full of pretzels and washed them down with beer. As a result, he became thicker. Gerda and the children could barely be tolerated. Their obtrusiveness began to irritate him, especially after an exciting day at school. At bedtime, he'd stretch out, bored.

"Ugh, I'm so full!"

"You shouldn't eat too much of that stuff," Gerda replied.

"Put you it me or not."

"Surely you must possesses some self-control, I suppose?"

Instead of a reply, he gave her a withering glance. Her reaction was predictable.

"What is this miserable existence?" he asked.

"We're not all bad. Everybody lives like us."

"What does that matter?" was his powerless defense, "we get drunk to prosperity. Every day is like the previous one. A person needs variety and distraction."

"What then? Would you want to compromise your status?"

"For my part," he growled in the absence of a rebuttal.

During a conversation with his colleagues, a folder was pushed into his hand. This leaflet was found by a group of unsprayed Indians who practiced Eastern mysticism under the guidance of a guru. Tony's interest was piqued. He decided to take the course. One thing led to another. After three years, he has learned enough to give limited group lessons himself. Once evening a week, he would set up in an old school. He also placed an ad in a newspaper. Enough participants signed up to cover costs. After two years, he was able to delve deeper in the mysticism. He was able to completely fill a second night. Eventually, he stopped when he had enough money over to buy a small summer house in a village on the IJsselmeer where his boat was parked.

In better times, Aisha and Han never went to the same place for a second time. They wanted charm. During a cruise in the Aegean, they spent one of their days on the island of Santorini.

"This looks like a suitable place to spend our last days," he had remarked at the time.

Now, an ample occasion presented itself.

At the airport of Hellinikon Athens, the flight to Santorini was an hour late. He had sufficient time to quietly drink an espresso. On the way to the buffet, Han dodged someone carrying a full tray of drinks. It suddenly occurred to him that he had promised to let the likeable Belgian hear something. This was a good reason to send him a card. Afterward, in the plane on the way to his destination, he thought of that last period before the final departure from his hometown. Does it make sense to worry about it?

The plane, a De Havilland, was occupied by a dozen people. Han sat next to a Greek lady who had two Siamese cats. During the flight to Mykonos, a stopover had had to be made. One of the cats went on Han's knee. He stroked its velvet coat and the friendly animal sat snugly on his lap. His thoughts came back to the lost time. At that time, Aisha and he love their conjoined twins Mau-Mau and Geisha. About three years ago, they moved the cats to Elysium. Aisha had their remains buried next to the gazebo.

Three minutes later, the aircraft landed at the small airport of Mykonos. The Siamese got out along with their owner. After a short time, the plane made a perfect landing on the sandy Santorini Airport. Han had to wait half an hour for a taxi to go to the town of Fira. Santorini is a complex of islands, the two largest of which were Thera and Therasia. They were like a broken horseshoe enclosing a bay. In the bay of the womb is a trio of small islands. One of them, Nea Kameni, still exhibits low volcanic activity. From the harbor of main island of Thera, tourists are given the opportunity to make a trip to this island. It takes an hour to climb the crater, which hardly produces more than the smoke of a tobacco pipe. During the dusty walk around the caldera and descent to the jetty, the boat was to wait for the return of the tourists. The total complex of Santorini was the remains of an enormous volcanic eruption that came up in the past. The fatal eruption, which occurred about thirty-five centuries ago, crumbled the compact Santorini Island. According to some scientists, this burst led to the collapse of the Minoan civilization on Crete. The two large chunks of the volcano had a fertile layer of soil on their slopes that ran grainy towards the beaches of the surrounding sea. On the rock of the largest island of Thera was its capital, Fira. The central square of this small town is surrounded by shops, eateries, workshops, and the office of a bus company. Buses came and went and services were maintained in the village and harbor areas hundreds of feet below. There's a small dock for yachts and fishing boats, and the trip to the crater island started there. The quay, with a single restaurant, also served as a landing stage for passengers from the cruise ships that entered the bay at anchor. Fira is only accessible via a donkey ride through a zigzagging path in the rock. The arduous journey took about half an hour. The taxi took Han from the airfield to the high square of Fira. In a tobacco store, he bought a map. The shopkeeper if he here briefly a rolling cart parking. In a narrow side street, he climbed the stairs to the main level. This street had no traffic and there was a row of houses that made the view panoramic. The panorama made Han feel overwhelmed. Speechless, he leaned over the railing to the end of the precipice. "This is where I want to return in order to rest and lick my wounds," he thought. "The sea twinkles in the afternoon as if it's forgiven me. Pearls emerge from the deep for a moment before dissolving back to sea again. The volcanic island floats like a fuzzy jewel. The golden sun colored the sea and the water reflected the sky."

In the distance lay Therasia, the other big island. The bright sunlight lit the white village houses.

The color change that was recreated in the rock layers of dominant island of Thera made it feel like a living organism, a kind of chameleon that had a palette of shades in its epidermis. Nearby in the background of the main street stood the Cathedral of Fira. It was a rhythmic architectural marvel of simplicity. The sunlight reflected its blinding white color. It was a pristine location to pray. No contemporary structure could compare to the natural scenery of that rock. Han broke away from the fascinating spectacle and walked down the street in search of a hotel. A hundred yards along the path, he came upon Hotel Panorama. The hotelier led him to a single room that overlooked a courtyard. After Han had picked up his suitcase at the tobacconist, he went to settle down. He put his pants and shirts in the wardrobe and distributed his underwear and socks and shoes under the cabinet. He put his shaving kit and other toiletries on the dressing table in the bathroom.

When everything was arranged to his liking, he climbed the four short steps to the bare restaurant at street. He bought two bottles of cold beer at the bar. Back in his room, he put the bottles in the small fridge. After a refreshing shower, he dozed in bed for an hour. Afterward, he sat on the balcony and drank beer, enjoying the panorama of the volcanic landscape as he flipped in the guidebook. By eight o'clock, he strolled the main street in the direction of a busy restaurant that consisted only of a terrace. He sat at a table near the railing and ordered a simple dinner with a bottle of chilled retsina. The terrace empty. Han quietly drank the remainder of the wine while enjoying the panoramic view of the sea. He could not get enough of it.

After a long exhausting day, evening came. Slowly, the sky became purplish pink dome over the bay. The world seemed to glow from within. The entourage gave him an inner peace, a peace one experiences when one's expectations are exceeded. A bright idea came to Santorini as to his next possible destination. There are certain things he'd need to do last as the undeniable charm has illustrated. Nature is relentless. Our appearance and disappearance can happen in less than one incident. The grains of sand that have washed up on the beach are at the time swallowed up by the sea of eternity. No shadow of mind will ever be lost in the existence and we'll know nothing more. That was Han's philosophication. He leaned on both elbows and with his hands on the stone balustrade, he stared out to the horizon, lost in his mind. The vague volcano world had encased him under the bright galaxy.

Two weeks after Aisha's confidences, a meeting was scheduled between the stakeholders. In those two weeks, Han wasn't able to fully concentrate on his work. They avoided each other. Small business issues were done through the staff. During meals, they casually made brief remarks. The atmosphere was abstract and distant.

Han managed to control himself. He avoided the subject of yoga. Tuesday afternoon. He remarked Aisha's nervousness, as well as her restless glances at the clock. She was preparing to leave for the capital. Her hands were sweaty. After dinner, she filled the dishwasher and moments later, she left with the sports car. Han left his job in the lurch. He had almost lost all interest in it. He washed his hands and dressed up. He thought as he paced in the lounge. Unrest overpowered him. Finally, he left the house and looked for a café near the vicinity. The group of people there were known pub tigers: a group playing billiard, a couple that needed to relax, and the batsmen that only had a few drinks. Han involved himself in a conversation with someone in a bar. However, it distracted him little from his misery. The shadow of his suspicions regarding Aisha loomed over him. The following Friday after Aisha's departure, he tried to find some fun in another pub. He saw the same audience. He had the same trivial conversations that Tuesday evening. Han drank his beer and strolled at the beach. The weather was bad. In the hope that his unrest would soon blow away, he walked under the freshening storm.

After an hour, on the way back, his spirit was overgrown by his fantasies. She'd arrive later at around ten o'clock. The thought that someone was taking her away from him harassed him. Jealousy.

Jealousy is an archaic trait. Are we still primeval men or Neanderthals? Can someone be considered as private property? The yoga haunts him. In an effort to control himself, he began to walk faster. Finally, he ran along the beach. The storm raged and plaintive chords moaned through the blowholes of the dune. Han tripped and fell from fatigue. He hit the dune and he remained lying there, exhausted. His heart pounding, he was soon short of breath. His face contorted to unplanned tears. What does it mean to live without? What is important?

The thoughts stammered his mind. He was filled with self-pity and bitterness. Where would he go? He grew desperate.

"Aisha," he whispered to the wet sand, "Why are you doing this to me?"

"Be wise and put an end to it. That will remove all obstacles," the wind howled through his head.

How? And then what? Only the void was before him! He knew he'd need fortitude and willpower. Once the "how and what" was discussed, the impulse would be over. This tedious philosophizing calmed him down a little. His breathing became regular again now that he was no longer galloping across the sand. His watch was nearly half an hour past ten. He wanted to be home before she arrived at eleven o'clock. With a deep sigh, he wanted to rid himself of all pathos. He stood up. He patted the sound out of his pants and leather jacket. With a sleeve, he wiped some sand from his face. Exhausted, he arrived home. On the first floor was a light in the lounge. Aisha, who was sitting with a magazine, was having a drink. Her knees were raised in a corner of the sofa. She marveled at his haggard appearance.

"Why do you look like that!? What have you been doing?" she asked.

"I fell on a sand dune," he muttered. For the first time in a long time, she showed interest in him.

"What are you looking at me quizzically for?"

He remained silent.

"I was already back at half past eight," she shared, almost casually. "The lesson was canceled. I forgot. There was a birthday or something."

Han nodded. How long had it been since she was so talkative? He took his jacket off and washed his hands and face in the bathroom. His absent behavior seemed to disturb her. She sniffed at him. Silently, he searched his room. Afterward there was not returned to the incident.

The next morning, he woke up just as his alarm clock tuned off. He saw the boxes of Vesparax and a glass of water. "Don't rush it," Han's mind said at first glance, "If I'm tired, I'll crush the tablets, mix them with yogurt, and drink it down. Then, I'll wake up feeling painless, hassle-free, and fit." It was a reassuring thought and a perfect solution. After shower and breakfast, he sauntered over to the cathedral. "Ypapantis tou Sotiros" said a white sign next to the entrance. He went inside. Near the entrance he dropped a hundred drachmas in a box. He then took ten thin candles. Cautiously, he lit one and put the slim stick in a dispenser. With every candle, he waited attentively and watched their burning light. He also lighted a candle in the inner chamber with a certain reverence for the mystery of fire. With this ritual, he said a silent prayer for the dead. He was devoured by the gaping maw of eternity.

Father Marcus Wolff was gassed in the concentration camp.
"Humanity is ordered on the earth."
Sjouke's mother was unable to warm herself.
"Nothing ever comes from you,"
Victor Hauser, an older friend. "Too bad. You're right."
Frits van den Wijngaart said, taking a photo, "Is my dick well?"
Simon van Straten, eternal loser.
"Goochem and melon chem."
Hans Naarden, the meek.
"On my apples, I know how your pear flavors."
Kurt Ruprecht, Soldat Freundlich.
 "I do not mean any harm."
Hans Rooy Earthy, a painter with four girlfriends.
"It tends to be a little too much."
Boy de Haas, who just rose from his death.
"Being beautiful isn't everything."
Aisha.

At the time, he wanted to flash the kernel and put the candle. He suddenly pulled his hand back as if he had been burned. "What now?" he pondered. "I'm not doing voodoo! Why do I remember her? Let her live as she wants. Let her be happy." He sighed and shook his head. How do you stay away from the past? Can the memories be filtered so that only the pleasant ones remained in the screen of your mind? Would we be who we are now? Or we wouldn't be more vulnerable than children, devoid of any kind of history? Thoughtfully, as if his luck was involved, he put the tenth candle on the stack. "Maybe I can make it clear in another life, if there is one, or in another dimension if one exists." He had serious doubts about that and shrugged. But you never know. "Good luck, Aisha. I still love you," he thought despairingly. Then, in an attempt at self-reflection: "The desire for your heat is an honest one if it was not mixed with the need to be able to be with myself. Even without you, you still stand in the way. We are entwined in a web of affections in which sense is often no more than an illusion of self-love. Happiness teeters on the razor's edge. We could lose everything in the next moment. Be careful. Happiness requires talent. My talent for happiness is one of brooding. What should I do with it? A sober person must be able to settle down in the facts, circumstances, and inability." He stared at the tableau of burning candles which occasionally flared as an organ's sound resonated. "In due time, will someone light a candle for me? Alas, that isn't the point," he mused. It was of no importance. "You do what you do either from a whim or because you are in a milder mood. Is that why we are only on vacation when we walk into a church? So we can experience silence? The aesthetic experience is an excuse especially in a place where we don't belong."

He withdrew from the ritual and strolled in his mind. He lost interest in the pompous altar and the painted walls. Han knew few biblical connotations:

"Vanity of vanities, vexation of the spirit..."

Possibly the best buttress for each faith is unbelief as an excuse for doubt. He mused as he sauntered towards the exit. Yet, each man has his own form of mysticism. He got bored and shrugged. Mysticism is mystification, he decided soberly. But still...

From the twilight of the porch, the day entered. It was overwhelming! The blazing sun burst in an eruption of light and heat. Blinded, he groped for his sunglasses in the breast pocket of his shirt. On the right side of the street stood the old houses that have been jointly drilled. Opposite them was the balustrade with the panoramic view. The maritime landscape was now a lovely veil. It was as if it was trying to protect the islands against the aggression of the sun. Nea Kameni, (a partially submerged, slumbering cinder-skinned beast which incessantly exhales yellow, sulfur vapor and gas), Palea Kameni, Aspronessi, and more to the right of the untouchable big chunk violated horseshoe, Therasia Island.

"The light shines on both good and evil without discrimination or judgment. And everything and everyone is doing his advantage," Han said in a timid attempt at profundity.

Between the main street of Agios Ypapantis and the lower street of Agios Minas was the shaded terrace of "Victors." On the one hand, it was accessible via staircase. It was carved into the hard rock. On the other side ran a narrow shopping street. The place was peppered with refreshments. It offered a splendid view of the place, as well as some classical music. The guests were treated to the sounds of a piano piece by Satie. Han was not fond of Satie. He regarded his pieces as an introduction to more work, and there was hardly anything.

He took a free table by the railing. A spirited waitress took his order. Her name was Melissa, since the name was written on her body, or so he thought. Melissa was like a baby, young, slim, and still keen. A lone man around her could possibly get rid of her melancholy for a short while. She made Han's mood lighter. The text of the postcard, which he had recently sent to the Fleming, occurred to him:

Men are like matches
They suddenly flare up
then lose their head.

"What about women?" he wondered skeptically.

On one of those overheated days, he took a walk along the sea. Beyond the bottleneck of the island lay under, a canopy of bones, the walls and heaps of the time buried town of Akrotiri. Since the sixties, archaeologists have been startled at its secrets, and tourists ruined its thirty-five centuries of peace. A student asked him if he knew why the ruins were always so broken and dusty. Han grinned and was reminded of a statement by James Joyce: "The rubble of time builds houses of eternity."

A day later, he rode a bus to the quiet beach of Perissa. He swam in the clear water and stayed there for a short time amidst other people. He also sunbathed at the beach. Soon, he was chased by the flaming arrows of Helios to the small beach restaurant. In this establishment, the temperature was reasonable compared to the hot casserole outside. He chose a fish dinner from the modest menu. The innkeeper served him a bottle of ice cold retsina and after a short time, served him a delicious baked trout. Han suspended his departure as heat became worse and ordered a second bottle. Despite enjoying the peace and the wine, his slightly tipsy mind lingered to the coast of the past.

Without exchanging a word of their thoughts on the upcoming meeting, they drove to the coffee shop of Pronk under the Carlton Hotel in their small sports car. They were going to meet Tony.

The two people had too much to say to be able to articulate it in a peaceful atmosphere. Tony wasn't there yet. Aisha and Han took the opposing position and ordered two espressos with the usual glass of water. To an outsider, it looked like a cozy gathering. A second glance would reveal to them that both people avoided eye contact as much as possible. Han put a lump of sugar in his coffee and asked:

"That friend of yours… What did I actually miss?" At the same time, he seemed to know the answer: youth and vigor. To his amazement, it was something else.

"Attention," she said.

"Is that really necessary?" Was his quick reaction.

Aisha shook her head and sighed.

"You'll meet him later."

"We've been married over fourteen years and you don't want to talk?"

"You had the chance. You were married with your work over the years and now it's too late. What could you expect otherwise?"

"You also stood behind and planned in building a financial cushion so we could stop working at a short notice. I don't understand you! We have everything! A large stock portfolio, a good life, a Mercedes sports car, a big house, we're healthy, you name it! You have closets full of clothes but always wear that sweater and jeans. You can buy what you want. You did not want children. You claimed that a child is the product of lust and I ensured we wouldn't have one. Every year we go on a holiday in a five star hotel abroad!"

"Once a week a year to ski the last two years," she interrupted him scornfully, "It's always the same."

"That could now do about it."

"And even then it was not possible for you to relax. Before you could settle down, you wanted a few days away. I can still hear you say, 'What am I doing here when I should be busy at home?' And you know it. Therefore, all our vacations are irrelevant."

"Is that all? Is that the ultimate reason for all of this?"

"One of the reasons. How long have we been living in discontent? You always come to the same conclusion. As if that's sufficient. And indeed, that's enough. More than enough."

"What reason do you need? I want to know," he stubbornly maintained his arguments.

"Oh, so much. The key is love..."

"Love?" He looked at her in surprise. He noticed himself and thought of the cliché.

"Yes, love." She continued. You won't understand it. I wonder if you even know what that means."

"You dare pretend as if you have a patent on it?" His index finger pointed in her direction.

"Don't make a scene. We'll attract attention. This is a pointless discussion. Let's stop this."

He pulled the gesture back and got himself under control.

"As you wish," he growled sullenly and aggrieved.

It did not make sense at this time. In this situation, in this atmosphere, he understood. Maybe she's right. Earnings can't force love. He drank some of his espresso. He could see her expression and he realized that behind his back, her lover had entered.

Tony, a tall blond young man, pulled a chair and sat down beside Aisha as if he belonged there.

Challenged with bravado, Han observed the man. The boy was young enough to be his son. He had a certain charm that made him so entrancing. In fact, he makes a soft impression. How could the boy have won over his wife? Compared to how the couple opposite him looked, Han felt old.

"So," Tony said, embarrassed, "Here we are. My name is Tony."

"Yes," she agreed and looked at him with a longing gaze.

Han can't free himself of his jealousy to the point where his insides are essentially screaming: YOU'VE BETRAYED OUR LOVE AND FRIENDSHIP!

However, he still loved Aisha. She was his great love. Love is a superior emotion that can go one-way. With love, you can haggle. Love is flexible. Friendship implies equivalence. Your wife can cheat when it comes to a relationship or sex habit. Where love and friendship go together, that's not possible. He thought he knew Aisha, and now he no longer has her. A man is composed of ephemeral thoughts and affections. He should be careful with what he does and with what he feels. "Too wide Feld," he told himself though it was essentially nothing more than a form of self-protection.

"Han. Is your wife coming? The agreement was that she would also be here," he feigned in astonishment.

"No," Tony stared at him, struggling to keep his face straight; as if he wanted to measure the older man. "She's busy, and we weren't able to find a babysitter."

Han held his gaze and could not escape the impression that the boy was lying. "Too bad for you!" he thought. "I can easily call your wife and ruin you."

In the course of the one-sided conversation with the other two, he did not clearly know exactly what they were planning.

"We'll see,"

"I see nothing," Han responded strongly to the wezienwelitis.

"It's possible that you did not notice, but by chance I am more or less interested if uhh... husband... shall we say. Still. "

"You do know that I want to leave?" Aisha snapped. "I want to rent a room as soon as possible, or maybe a little house in the city. Tony's arranging his divorce with Gerda. Right?" She turned to him. Tony nodded absently.

With that nod, Han felt his toes curl. Do they want to announce it so publicly? He glanced at Tony who carelessly. He wanted to get rid of his supporters. He acted as if there were no women or children at risk. Han suddenly noticed that he was clinging to each emerging thought in his head. What would help him?

"And what about our divorce?" he asked, seemingly interested.

Aisha looked disturbed.

"You can still arrange that..."

"Aha," he thought. "I just learned they came to this conclusion. Tony's support and presence was necessary for her. Is this the finely tuned Aisha I've stayed with for so long? Was it all an illusion? How can an amazing woman change so quickly? Is it because she is in love? That must be the explanation! What could I do?" In an impotent rage, he could barely suppress the thoughts that swept over him.

"I..." he responded aggressively. With a bewildered look, he pressed a hand to his chest, "I rule nothing. Who wants to leave? You, or me?" he snapped. With the thought of the emotional damage he would suffer thereby, he was not going in their interests by going through the hassle of the divorce. In that respect, he lacked sportsmanship and energy. Why should I be sporting in this case?

His opponents gave him hardly any attention. For them, the conversation had ended. They chatted a bit about yoga that evening. It seemed as if the only thing that existed was yoga. No concrete agreements were materialized. He felt superfluous and thought about things. Through his indignation and anger, he no longer felt able. "Nevertheless, I'll manage to bring an understanding of the real situation. Verbal communication is equal to anti communication and leads to misunderstanding. Communication through language is multi-interpretable. But it's too complicated. We don't say what we mean and we don't mean what we say. Our access has been locked together for the lack of good will, or whatever it may be. And what then? Would we have something else? Empathy? I don't know. I don't understand these, Aisha," he thought in his despair and rebellious mood. "I still love you. I can't strip my feelings for you." He sighed and his heart sank in his shoes. He again felt pressure on his stomach. "Everything I bring an argument forward, it goes against me. All I can come up with are arguments of God himself. The sentence is passed on without having the defendant a chance to plead his case due to the selfishness of his judges. That sentence also applies to the absent 'Third in the League'" considered Han. The lack of interest of the couple in front of him also meant an intuitive sympathy for Gerda. "Weak brothers support each other," he thought cynically and glanced sideways. The dark diamond beside him reflected a tired fifty year old man. "How many people have I worn to get this far? Time escapes you and leaves you behind, withered. I won't give up because of her. It shouldn't come to this! He has no regrets about this. If it beeps him, I beep him, he decided. "You don't just love a woman because of her qualities, you also love her despite her imperfections! Although that may go too far, how far is too far? That is a failure of love."

The stereo in the coffee shop suddenly suffered from an internal terror. A woman's voice sang the withered hit, "The Winner Takes It All." You can't lose a bit, the loser loses all. Han tried to create some order in the chaos of his thoughts and was skeptical in. Order is fiction. He considered it to be a fringed phenomenon. Order depends on absurdity. Order is like a stray snowflake in the desert. We are embedded in chaos and try to classify it as the inscrutability of God, an accident, or circumstances, or the law of nature and other causalities. Every choice meant the relinquishing of all other possibilities' freedom. One choice isn't the solution. The question is whether or not there could be another solution. Every time you are confronted with new facts, which are recorded the previous. There are no solutions. For it is as it is and not otherwise. There will always be victims who get the debris imputed. In this case, the wife and children of Tony, and himself. Everything ends in impotence and disintegration. Han rose dejectedly up and went to the toilet. Aisha and Tony took advantage of the opportunity to kiss each other.

By the weekend, Han rode in the heat of the bus to Oia, the northernmost village on Santorini. Oia had the rarefied atmosphere that the painter Meinema had painted so smoothly and aptly portrayed.

He rented a room from an old woman who lived in one of the many dilapidated whitewashed houses. There was a clean bed, a wooden table with a chair, and in the corner was a bowl and ewer on a deck. In a niche with lockable door, he could store some of his clothes. Most of his luggage was in Hotel Panorama.

The next morning at the crack of dawn, he went to meet the sunrise with a camera. The island complex was shrouded in mist. The air, land, and water formed a unity of sparkling life. In the diffuse twilight, there was virtually nothing to perceive other than the roar of the sea and the cries of flying birds. For some time, he sat on a rocky point and breathed the silence in. The atmosphere seemed tangible. It had taken hold of him and he intensely enjoyed the place. "I am still capable," he considered.

Suddenly, a beam of light rays broke the mist. The new day has arrived. Click... click... click... his camera just went on.

Later in the morning, he strolled through the narrow streets and alleys along the fractured teeth of dilapidated houses. He stepped inside a pub and drank raki with the natives. He ordered breakfast and coffee. Someone tried to strike up a conversation with him. Two men in a nearby group knew some English and German words. The conversation, however, was limited to a kink or a good-natured smile.

After this break, he explored photographing the vicinity of the village. By noon, the tourist flow started. The majority of the tourists consisted of students loitering around the perimeter. In the afternoon they returned to their base in Fira by bus. Fir is a beach town on the other side of the island.

Han lingered for a few hours in the shade with his back leaning against a crumbling wall. He gazed at the twinkling stars and the dancing water. The vague islets were in the distance. His mind sought the shelter of his youth and adolescence; to the time when he was still single. And of course, he was happy for years with Aisha. The previous stage was an overture. He sighed. "My most prized possession, my love, I have not paid sufficient attention to you because of a fixed idea. I've wasted my time. Happiness is most appreciated when it's over."

His intense desire to see Aisha at one point became so dominant that the unrest almost had him overpowered. "What am I doing here? I have to leave here." The sweat broke out. He stood up and looked around wildly as though he was looking for a way out. "Where should I go? There is no way out. Yes, this is the final end. We shall see."

Before he could move on to some disordered activity due to his anxiety, he was able to control himself. "Was there a better place on earth anywhere?" He considered the possibility. I will never be able to find peace in a similar mood. Everywhere else, Aisha is distant and unreachable. "She owns me and she dwells in me. I am a stranger to myself among strangers. I'll have to get used to it even if it means a revolution. This place is good or bad. As long as we are in the world, we have to be somewhere. Also, that logic is flawed." He distanced himself from the thought. The unrest drew the first rain of autumn slowly. A sigh of wind came from nowhere and tempered his violent emotion. "Apparently, the heat has thinned my blood. Every effort requires energy." He sat back in the same place and closed his eyes. Despite the dark sunglasses, he got tired of the heat and bright light. After some time, his mind floated away to solitary wanderings again. An unprecedented form of existence took possession of him. For some time, he basked in this unknown condition and felt secure.

On a nearby square, the horn of a group of tourists sounded. It was time to depart. The horn brought Han back to reality. He felt calmer now. Gradually, the temperature became bearable. He looked at the boats that sailed into the bay from the north.

"This seems an appropriate place to stay a little longer," he considered. "I'll go to Fira before I move permanently to this village. I'll stay here for a few weeks. I have enough reading material and photographs. The idleness is becoming less curious for me. Can I get it myself? I want out, then I'll swallow the Vesparax. Life and death has a covenant with me and they inhabit the same house."

After meeting Tony in the coffee shop, they drove back to their home. They had no words for each other. Both were busy in their own thoughts and their entangled emotions. Moreover, Han had to pay attention to the traffic during rush hour. When they were finally driving on the highway, he asked:

"What are your plans for tomorrow?" He tried his voice to sound as neutral as possible.

"What do you mean? What I always do on Tuesday. Go to yoga."

Han shook his head and gave her a dismissive look.

"I think I will not tolerate that." Essentially, he meant that he could not handle it emotionally.

"How come? Since when do you tell me what to do?"

"Since now." His voice was measured and he looked at her, somewhat challenging to her. "We're still married. You'll have to follow certain standards from now on. Have I ever gone on an outing? You leave constant questions. As long as we live together in one house, we will both do yoga together." The latter sarcasm was accompanied with a wry smile. "You want to leave, so what are we waiting for?"

"Ridiculous. You can't turn on the pavement like a pack of old newspapers. It is also my home. You can't force anything on me."

"I can't? Weren't you the lady with the civilized, sensitive nature? Or is your compass upset? Do you even think my situation, if only for a few seconds? Give me a little empathy.

That yoga guru in the capital won't blame you. And if so, then that's your problem."

"It's not clear to me what you mean." She squinted at him. Her violet eyes twinkled in her furious ivory face. She had immediately understood what he meant. That was the dilemma. The formulation and irony had hurt her. Behind him were hidden emotions he could barely control. She understood afterwards. Now, Tony was missing in her company. Both were silent for a short time.

"That's nonsense," she broke the silence with feigned displeasure. "I'll be the wisest and temporarily with my mother revoke, this banal squabbling not to drive the striker. "

Han silently agreed. Moments later, he asked:

"Does mother know?"

"She knows nothing. I imagine that she has a fait accompli. Are you satisfied now?" she snapped.

"It will take the fun out of it," he taunted.

"That's your problem," she hissed. She sounded very sharp. "It's disgusting. It's like the bickering of a cat and a dog."

"I'm not the one to blame here," he kept his other words back. Of course it's his fault. Sadly, enemies should split. All circumstances have been sad.

When they returned, one of the girls closed the case. Aisha immediately began to pack her paraphernalia in four suitcases and bags. When she was finished, she called her mother.

"Mom? I'm staying for a few days. "

"Why child?"

"I'll tell you when I'm with you."

"By yourself?"

"Yup. Han is too busy with his work."

"You're so curt. Is everything alright between you?"

"There isn't... there isn't anything between us. I'm coming soon and then you'll hear everything."

"Child, what's the matter? Is it serious?"

"Well, no. Mom, don't worry. See you later."

"Yes, but..."

"Okay. I'm leaving immediately. Goodbye, Mom." She broke the connection quickly to avoid further awkward questions. That would be addressed soon enough, she thought justly.

Han was in the bathroom freshening up. The door was ajar. He walked down the stairs to the workshop. Moments later, appeared Aisha.

"What will do you do with the staff?" she formally said.

"That's no longer your concern. I will do what there is to do here. They've been working hard," he growled.

"Tomorrow morning, I'm going to your mother's."

Aisha wandered through the rooms, hesitant. She seemed like she was saying goodbye in the home she had been happy for in many years. She came back again to the door of the workshop. Her face had the expression of a petulant child.

"Well then. I'm going," she sullenly said.

"Go," he muttered dryly without looking at her. His head spun. It was pointless to make her change her mind. Or maybe it was less pointless than he has guessed? With a cramped car and a head full of uncertainty, she started the car and went to the capital. The next morning, Han drove with a neighbor to Amsterdam. He took the cart that was parked in front of her mother's door. To save the old lady a scene and sorrow, he did not make an appearance. As he drove away, he thought he heard a window close in the house.

On the bumpy road during the return trip from Oia to Fira, Han became inspired to take some pictures. "For what, for whom and why?" The only excuse he could rely on was because he can't resist the urge. The heat made him drowsy. His brain functioned too slowly. At the hotel room in Panorama, he took a bath, slipped between the sheets, and slept until seven o'clock. After supper, he lingered for some time in the restaurant and decided to go the local nightclub at Victor's.

During one of the many sunny mornings, Han strolled to the village of Firostefani. Along the way, he saw a photogenic church that had a soft terracotta hue. As he walked, he developed an appetite and at the tavern of Hotel Galini he ordered a modest lunch. He pondered why he still could not muster the energy to move permanently to Oia. He decided not to rush things. He thought the convenience of Hotel Panorama and its advantages. That afternoon, he walked back to Fira. The weather was very hot and the atmosphere was oppressive. He came along the terrace of Victors' and paused. Because of the thatch which filtered the sunlight, he the exotic atmosphere of the terrace. That noontime, there were only a few guests. The genre of music drew was generally for a staid audience. He sat down at a vacant table near the railing.

In fact, he realized, that people here often came in contact with their compatriots. Other than a stray student or an elderly couple on holiday in the inner city, the people don't interfere with you. They are quite acceptable and in his opinion, they are without conceit. Occasionally, he saw the Melissa the waitress serving the guests. At the table behind him sat two Germans who talked about their supper in deliberate hushed tones. The recorder sang "Vocalize" by Rachmaninov and then "Variations on Themes from Bellini La Somnambula" though Han was not sure. Or was it Glinka? Let it be both of them, he decided magnanimously

A meaningful emptiness overcame just as he had felt in recently in Oia before. The shadows of yesterday and tomorrow enveloped his thoughts. The guests behind him have already had dinner and their conversation dozed. The largest volcanic island of Nea Kameni was hidden from view. It lay like a thick omelet that simmered in the vibrant casserole bay. Everything was so in tune with Han's passivity that his heart threatened in giving up. He knowingly had to keep going. A void of pure nothingness overpowered him. It was as if time held its breath in anticipation of an epiphany. It was a somewhat exaggerated comparison perhaps, but this condition lasted for some time until someone in the group made a brief comment in a soft voice:

A feast for the eyes! "

Han's mind, which has been on other places for a number of days, was woken from his reverie.

The light behind the open entrance made her shine. She was abruptly overshadowed she appeared quite exquisitely as a slender woman. She had short, dark curly hair which distinguished her exoticism. She was simply but tastefully dressed in a fashionable summer dress. Her shapely legs were firmly in pumps with stiletto heels. They possessed the maturity of a Venus in her youth though one won't constantly recognize the request. In earlier times, it was suggested: "Someone with high taste." The attention of the guests was acutely focused on her. She had a grace that surpassed beauty, and that's according to Pascal's assertion. This was a correlation of both.

"Hello! Is this seat taken?" The deep sound of Aisha's voice betrayed her nervousness.

"Hello!" Han said, stunned. He rose to his feet. "Sit down," he introduced himself formally.

"Don't be silly," she responded as if they the situation was something to be a little shy about. She put her handbag and sunglasses on the table.

"What can I offer you?"

"Ice-cream-soda, please."

For a short period, both of them looked at each other's posture.

"Not in jeans?" He said. What a right way to get the conversation going!

"I never one wore when we went on holiday. You know that."

Another shortcoming.

"What about Buddhism?" He was unable to touch the chords to reach her. There was discrepancy between word and thought. It seemed as if his tongue was led by rancor. Without answering, she looked at him uncertainly. "I've converted to the Greek Orthodox faith," he continued with a smonzelende look at Melissa, who came to take the order.

Despite a slight irritation on this ambivalence, the girl smiled amiably as if a secret alliance between women existed.

"A sweet girl," she acknowledged once the waitress withdrew.

"How did it come about that you are on this side?" he said. He could not find the right formula to express himself delicately. "It's great to have you here!" Or was this banter an expression of joy over her unexpected arrival? She seemed teasing. That was possible. Or was it a matter of inability that put around him on injured self-love? It was too complicated, Han considered. This thought slid in the wings. She was no longer blinded by the love of Candlemas? She has recovered her innate distinction, he noted. This somewhat confused him.

"Will you stop being so annoying?" She managed to say in a neutral voice. "I'm alone," she said.

"Oh. Uh..." he hesitated, "Not on the road to Canossa?" Another blunder. He was irritably fixed on his clumsy setup like a basketball player who at every throw invariably just misses.

"Why do you have to make it so hard, Han?" she asked with a faltering voice. "Do you think it is nice to appear as a loser here?" She knew how to control herself.

Suddenly, he felt unstable. We're both losers, he considered. Something has changed. This affair has made her more accessible. In the homely atmosphere of her mother, she has apparently found time to reflect just as I have on this trip. Their eyes met. Her eyes sparkled as if tears were burning behind them. He realized he could not welcome her this way even though it was coming upon him.

"Okay..." it was as if his voice welled from a deeper layer of his soul. He put a hand on hers. "Can happen what would, in my opinion you will never be the aggrieved party there... '

"And that it's also revealed," he wanted to add. He felt that time wasn't an issue and abandoned the idea. At the same time, he wondered whether or not this approach required him to abandon his plan to stay in Oia. Something like regret streamed in his thoughts which overran their complexity. Should he abandon his independence? Was it worth it? Will he miss the misery of freedom? It was something like an alibi that could break together a welcomed partner. Or was is it self-torture? "Farewell earth, Farewell sky." Monteverdi's comments echoed on the tape recorder. Chance has occasionally interesting aspects in store, he observed.

Melissa approached and served the refreshments. Han's eyes wandered towards the lovely Aisha. Mandatory beauty... She smiled. She has again gotten a hold of herself. And him. It was as if they shared the same thoughts, as if there was no longer a border conflict between them that existed like a telephone where an the unknown witnesses is having an intimate conversation. She smiled again. Does she have an idea of my split personality? Is she already convinced of the end result?

"If I had not been sure of it, I would not have looked," she acknowledged, after Melissa had moved away. Han was able to get his last words out with some difficulty.

She has a high opinion of me. Too high. I'd rather not know. That's frustrating. It'll only put me back to the chopping board. That's less enjoyable. Obligations grow. Can it be impossible to continue? That's not fair. There are few words that can make this contact short. And even less to restore it, as shown.

To his amazement, he was not happy about her coming despite her transformation.

"You aim well," he remarked as neutrally as possible and slid his previous thoughts temporarily into the background. He did not talk again.

"It's wasn't easy. No one knew where you were going." She seemed a little relieved.

"I said nothing to anyone," he muttered. "How did you know?"

"A hunch. I called the man who has taken over the case. "

"Have you met him?" he interrupted her.

Aisha pulled her mouth wide and shook his head. She out her sunglasses back on and watched the dancing glare of the bay which reflected in her green / brown lenses. It was as if her eyes shot a private universe. He took a sip from his glass.

"I told you so that you could pick up everything."

"It did not happen. Moreover, where could I leave it? "

"He's jovial man. Flemish is a Burgundian. He looks like a huge sausage stuffed with hamburgers, croquettes, meatballs, potatoes, pretzels, cherries, and juicy stories," he chuckled.

"When I phoned him, he had received a card from you a few days ago saying you were on your way to Santorini."

"You have to put something on a card. When did you call?"

"The day before yesterday. I promptly booked with a travel agent. An hour later, the trip was arranged."

"That's hot News! You got a regular flight?"

"Yesterday morning, I flew to Athens and stayed overnight at the Stanley Hotel. This morning, I left Hellinikon. I landed here a few hours ago."

"You were lucky! I had to wait a week before I could fly from Athens to Santorini. During that time, I spent three days in Delphi and purchased a comrade." He took the round ball owl from his pocket and showed it to her. "He's called Therapon."

"Brother in arms? Can I have him?"

Han put the little owl on the table and grinned ironically: "He's a comrade against the emptiness of existence."

Aisha gave him a questioning look. She took the owl in one hand and admired the capricious Onyx structure.

"What a sweetheart. He looks so…" She made a wry face. She held her mouth down like a Japanese woodcut by Sharaku. Han was charmed. She was now in an excellent mood. Apparently, she was pleased of his modified arrangement.

"The Belgian's new knowledge."

"I could directly book a night's stay in Athens in Amsterdam," she continued the conversation and put the owl back on the table.

"Why the rush?"

"I was suddenly worried on a whim."

"Worried? About what?"

"About that. I'll tell you in due time, perhaps."

He wondered what it could be but he did not insist anything.

"Where's your luggage?"

"At the reception at Hotel Panorama."

"How did you know I was staying there?"

"I've been through two hotels. At the Panorama, someone at the front desk knew that you were here. They showed me the way. Everyone was friendly and helpful."

"I can imagine. I have a single room. The hotel is fully booked," he teased, grinning good-naturedly, "Maybe the Kavalari or Hotel Galini has a room available."

Aisha lowered her sunglasses slightly on her nose and looked at him slyly. He knew that she knew that he was twisting the truth; that he left marks in the way. It was one of his typical features. He knew her from before; relaxed, amiable and charming.

"How did it all run?" He asked the question in passing and let his gaze cross the water to the distance to give her space for an evasive answer. To his surprise, she answered straightly.

"A week or two before you called Schiphol, I basically had enough. It was a drunk infatuation. I sat for a while with myself back in a knot on the road. A kind of failure for my nerves. I found it hard to get back at your groveling. I felt mortified..." Aisha hesitated before she continued her story. "He insisted from the outset to have sex. I felt it was still too early to go to that stage. But still. He was a man who wants to hang out and a bachelor who needs to be taken care of."

"Did he have to stay with his mother?" The words escaped Han, not devoid of resentment.

"Well, his wife Gerda was a troublesome child."

"And he would divorce her?"

"Yes, that and other things. I don't regard divorce as decisive. He wanted time to continue. After all, he had obligations to his family. It all happened so quickly. He wanted to go to the direction of a free relationship. Well, that was the last thing I needed. From the day you put me out the door, I've repeatedly asked myself what I've been actually doing. I told Mom. She said, 'Call his wife again. She must know nothing.' That's exactly right. It was a lot of endeavor. Blame my address. I'd never done anything like that. I was fed up at the same time."

Han looked at her, aghast. That was what he had forgotten!

"What do you look?"

"I wanted to do it right after that meeting in the coffee shop." She said, her head thrown back. He drew out a breath and hit his hand on his knee. "Stupid, stupid, stupid! I should have immediately phoned his wife, as I had planned! It would have saved us a lot of trouble."

"Then we wouldn't be in all this nonsense. You were at work and remained the servant of your work and I was biting myself."

Han could not deny it. Although the turn of events gave him no reason to cheer.

"Well, he's not a bad man. Actually, he's more of a spoiled boy. Egocentric. He needs attention and care. I'm not the right type for him."

"No, you want attention," he chuckled, "And a nurse if possible!"

"If you know so well, why have you not done that in the last few years we've lived together?"

"Money, Aisha, money," he said loudly. Some guests turned their looks in their direction. He lowered his voice. "You know it by experience. Everyone, at some point, has been misled by their chimeras. I wanted to build a generous financial cushion, as you know. In recent times, I have had ample opportunity to reflect on a few things. It's become clear to me that we could live freely and safely with less than I'd imagined."

"What are your plans now?"

He hesitated. His eyes fell on the wedding ring on her slender finger.

"The case has been sold. I have no interest in it any longer."

"I know, but are you going to stay here?" She pursed her lips between two straws of ice-cream-soda. She was looking for an answer and he avoided her eyes and stared in the distance where the sun had put a robe of light in on the water.

"For some time over there..." he stammered as he pointed to the tip of the island with a nod. He was pointing at the village of Oia. "There's a quiet place with a view over the entire complex that I fancied. There are some dilapidated houses of former residents, and the stragglers who live there almost sleep the entire day. In summer, there's some tourism. The seasons pass quickly. I want, for the time being, to buy a house there." Hesitantly, he continued. "Until a time comes that I have known all the red tapes in my life and free myself of all restrictions..."

"I had a suspicion about that," she interrupted him. "Ever since I heard you were going to Santorini from that Belgian. Back then, when we spent a day here, you had already said that "This is a very nice place to spend the rest of my days." I know you a little Han, and I was afraid of you and your gloomy moods."

Her words shocked him. She's been worrying about him! What in heaven's name were they doing?

"Let us be silent about it," he dodged uncertainly, "Escaping life is a private matter."

"No, it's definitely not. You also have obligations to me. Remember Han, don't do anything stupid. Promise me..."

"You wanted to get rid of me," he interrupted. "The impression I gained at that time in that coffee shop was... well..."

"Nonsense, it's not as simple as that. You sent me away. But we did not part. You know that. We can start again. We'll make money together and..."

"Hoho," he protested as he lifted a hand, "that isn't currently being addressed. It isn't entirely clear to me whether I want to or not. You've attack me unexpectedly. You've soiled my faith in you. What guarantees me can you give me of our future, Aisha?"

"I acknowledge that I have made a serious mistake. It was a big mistake and I am truly sorry. Everyone makes mistakes. Haven't you made any mistakes? I've learned my lesson. Frankly, I don't understand why I did all that."

"The sackcloth disfigures men," he chuckled. "I have grossly neglected and you felt lonely. I recognized that too late. You're not the only to bear the blame."

"Last week, it's become clear what you mean to me to me, Han."

"That's not the point, Aisha," he dodged, "I also had time to think about a few things, as I pointed out earlier. The issue is about what we love, what we dream, were we want to live, and the situation we are in. There are too many to mention. You can be sure that I care for you. From the moment you stepped into the studio with Boy, I've found your personality to be that of a classy woman. All this taken into account does not mean that I want to be periodically put on the rack. Not by anyone."

"I absolutely don't expect you."

"Do it anyway, Aisha. Love isn't enough. Friendship requires seeing things from a higher order."

"Is that an obstacle for you to start with? Do you want my mate no more? Haven't we always been good friends? I think we've remained good friends despite our marriage."

"Outside our relationship, of course we are best friends..." he hesitated. This was not the most appropriate moment to discuss betrayal and friendship. But when could he talk about those things? "Look here, Aisha; let's start over with a clean slate. But not here. It's impossible. Something has happened that violated the both of us. And now, we're going to establish where we left off. The way I welcomed you is proof of that. I'm glad I saw you. Nevertheless, I could hurt my self-love not the boss. Those things are deeper than you suspect. You also need time to come at peace with yourself and to find your way back..."

Aisha could endorse his arguments. She regarded it as an excuse for his initial tough stance. She did not expect that he would receive her with open arms. She could spend this time hard to express herself. That was an inner, worldly atmosphere. She had hoped for the best. She knew Han all too well. She paused and sucked the last droplets of her drink from her glass. In his mind, he followed her actions.

"Let's think about it," he concluded after a pause, "You've made your proposal and this is mine. I know I've hopelessly failed. I can improve my life now that I'm no longer obsessed with work. Maybe we can still make something of it, maybe not. Only the future will tell."

Both of them were lost in thought. Their eyes wandered over the wide bay. Han's hand had again sought hers. It seemed as if their body parts had life of their own. Or was there something in advance in his mind that made the decision for him? He shook his head. The spirit and the human condition are an enigma which commonly can't come back. He drained his glass.

The sun was now past its peak. A light breeze extinguished the heat. It blew all over the terrace as the first notes of a fantasy overture by Tsjaikowskij played.

"Want something to drink?" He asked. His eyes searched Melissa to attract her attention.

"Let's," Aisha suggested. "I'm not in the mood for the grandiloquent drama of Romeo and Juliet."

"It has a few good notes. Okay, you don't even have a hotel. For tonight, you can go to my room. Grab your suitcase while I take a shower."

Her eyes met his, and they laughed together. He stood up and pushed his chair. She waited until he pushed her chair back as she stood up. She quietly walked to the exit. It was as if she was dancing through life. The looks of the guests followed her.

"Happy guy," muttered the German to his companion. Han paid Melissa the bill. His gaze followed Aisha. She was there! It made him happy at the moment. He sighed and mused to himself: "We adore our creations: gods, children, our work, a woman, and other illusions. These illusions seem commonly beautiful than reality. In any case, they make daily life bearable. However, the stay as illusions. Every living being is constituted in its own way to the world." Han turned to the lovely Melissa. Paying attention grows guilt he felt. "A man clears his obligations, including emotional ones, with gifts or money." He gave her a generous tip. The girl gave him a radiant smile and thanked him. On his way out, he has already forgotten her. A moment later he supported Aisha with an elbow as she climbed the stone steps to the main street.

In the hotel, he took her bags to the front desk. Han then took a shower. Meanwhile, Aisha stored her clothes and shoes at in her wardrobe and drawers. The toiletries were on the mirror in the bathroom.

After Aisha had taken a shower, there was still time before dinner.

"Shall we rest for an hour before we go again?" Han said with a dubious smile.

After they have merged into one another, Aisha crept like a purring cat close to him. His arm was around her while her dark head rested on his shoulder. The open balcony door let a stream of air in which kept the temperature of the rock chamber at tolerable levels.

"What are you thinking?" Aisha broke the period of silence. Usually, he felt overwhelmed with such a question. He usually felt like a child who has just been caught stealing sweets. Now, he had inward smile.

"I was considering the insanity of love and passion. What do you think?" he asked.

"Love is something that regulates infatuation into calmer waters. It has less ups and downs. It has little to do with reason or intelligence. Each man appears to love his way. Maybe there's one exception," she supposed.

"The first contact is made through observation, don't you think?" Meanwhile, he caressed the satin skin of her hip. "Would you someone to love his mind?"

"The visual is less important for me although I think that since our short separation, you look better. That idleness has done you no harm, friend."

"What is character?" he interrupted her. "In nature, you can certainly not build houses. Not even a bathhouse. Even on your own character, that is difficult. Sometimes, we do things that we're astonished of afterwards. That is why a character's description in a novel is nonsense. People are not puppets of their own nature. People act against nature and better judgment. That makes life so complicated and fascinating. What matters are the actions; the result of grabbing a bag full of impulses. In my opinion, that's the only criterion."

"You did not let me finish. A person's behavior towards me and others includes their charm, performance, and even clumsiness. All are reasons why you love someone or not. For example, tenderness or pity. Sometimes, even out of pity," she opined.

"Aren't we all side issues? This has the makings of an interview," he thought, grinning.

"The atmosphere surrounding a person's appearance can also be attractive. It has to do with charm as well as the intimacies you share together." She pressed her lips to his shoulder and, for illustration, bit gently. Han felt the treachery. "That is starting to become an obsession of mine. I must definitely put a line somewhere," he decided.

"And what do you think of passion?" he demanded.

"Passion is the expression of love."

"The fire and the end of love?"

She casually kissed him in his neck. "During the flight to Athens, I read in "The Mirror" about a long interview with a Russian ballerina," she continued. "They asked her how she thought about love. 'I often hear about but never say anything' was her answer."

Han laughed. They lay silently against each other for some time.

"How is it actually ended with the divorce that you would apply. Who passed or am I still uhh... vogue? He sniffed the fresh pine scent of her hairdo.

"I never requested divorce papers. I wanted a respite. That's what mom also recommended. I must not forget to call her."

"I thought of that back then but I heard nothing. Besides, filling out forms and answering letters was never your strong side."

Again, there was a silence in which the both of them wandered in the dense forest of their minds. Aisha suddenly rolled on top of him and her thighs tightened on his member. She kissed his eyelids.

"What we do now," she said neutrally, "Is something you or I want…"

Han burst out laughing and both bodies laughed.

"You committed blackmail only a female can," he said, hiccupping. His laughter was contagious, liberating. "What do you make of it?" he reflected as an accomplished social scientist, "You objected to 'Romeo and Juliette' and its dramatic ending." He gave her a kiss. "Let's sleep on it."

His gaze fell upon Therapon the owl which faithfully stood guard at the two boxes. All his life has been an unnecessary experience which made no sense. He mused, almost profoundly, that life sometimes offers an unbearable stench. Only the company of the other gives us a hint of interest. Together, they are rich. He took her in his arms and rolled her.

Han was awakened by morning light of the next day. He lacked the energy to get up. He put his hands behind his head and tried to sleep again. The thoughts escaped the cage of his consciousness which kept him from sleeping. He looked at Aisha, who slept with deep breaths. She was there again. They were together again. "The game may have changed slightly but the puppets are the same," he thought cynically.

What had been joy initially has now become gloom. He felt as if he had lost something. Was it his freedom of choice? Was the liberating feeling of freedom lost? Suddenly, it became clear to him. It was the indefinable charm of nostalgia! Aisha's arrival meant a hazy road between past and longing, melancholy, and wealth and loss was now blocked. Only the sweet memory of happiness remained. Was it is preferable than the tangible reality of the present moment? Was it more pleasant to live with desires than with facts? Desire was as much a reality and nostalgia in the form of self-deception. In daily life, the conscious and unconscious play with factors and phantoms along in the background so that we don't consume pure happiness. In those cases, reality appears more real than they should be in essence. He closed his eyes to see better. Was the only paradise to be reached a lost one? To his surprise, he was suddenly aware Aisha's advent was an anticlimax. Was he loyal to her? The universe of logic has many black holes from which empty moments leak from. There appears to be an area where reason has been stranded in shrivels of patina.

On the pillow next to his was Aisha's face. She held a slight smile towards him. Carefully, she scanned his eyes. She feels back at home. "I love all the women you've ever been," he said. "In part, you're my product as I am a product of you in part. As you are. I love you. Is it luck? I must be lucky. This moment will never repeat in the same context. I can emphasize that this is happiness. I feel it too. Happiness is such a large chunk to contain. When I say 'This is happiness,' it's the ratio of the happiness in the way, and it's already over. We could fix it if we wanted to. What kind of adjustments do we need? Is it something we should discuss? After this, there will only be less. With reminiscence, we might regain some of the past. The transient right now remains an obstacle; a reminder of an extremely poor reconstruction of reality. Falsification is desired in this case. However, it explains that almost all tangible reality goes against the principle of nostalgia. It idyll transcends the impossible. I wonder, can I still to this relationship?" He looked away.

He had reconciled with the thought in Oia. Now, it appeared that the way was blocked by the tyranny of the sense element! Aisha's presence explained the obligation to go on living; to be a hostage of love and his. While he had already crossed the fear of the last frontier, what came in its place? Was it the fear to continue living? No, not quite. Rather, it was something like apathy. "I was almost beyond death. Her arrival has crossed a line. Life is calling me to order. Now, I have to step out. I can do the impossible to her. I love Aisha and feel obliged to cultivate no guilt feelings. I cannot live without her and not with her. I welcome her return and feel sorry for the frustrated intentions. The fact is, this solution is now out of the picture. The disappointment! Is it depression? The road to the past is protected by the future. The days with her will consist of walking, sitting on a terrace, and lying on a beach intimately. This also applies when I choose a solitary life. Time will fill nothing. In the recent years, I have never considered this so closely. The emptiness that appeared yesterday is meaningful and has been stolen today. I can shoot pictures for a photo album and perhaps set up an exhibition. The secret of life is activities. And so what? Is activity also the secret of meaning? Does it all not matter? Money didn't prove to be the main motive as I thought, but it's what keeps us busy. I was a workaholic or, as they called it, the servant of my work. And now, am I to become the servant of my existence? That was enough for Aisha. And rightly so. What remains is my love for her. The problem is, can I spend the rest of my life with an upholster? Is that enough? Habituation is the worm of mutual love. It gnaws at "happiness." And that's in the most favorable case. Usually, it degenerates to annoyance and boredom. The fundamental issue is the quality of life. It's not an argument in favor of uniformity, drabness, or accidents. An artist will be willing or able to invest in something for the occasional accident to taste its fullness or to go on a masochistic streak. And they'd want to exploit it. What promise can I live up to our time together? What is the meaning of having a reminder on your side who has survived at some point? There remain questions whose answers I'm looking for; a typical case of disease prosperity." He yawned of apathy. His eyes wandered to the open balcony doors. On the nightstand stood a glass of water. He took a sip of lukewarm water because his throat was dry. He put the glass back and came face to face with the grumpy owl, the guard who watched over the Vesparax. They stared at each other for some time. Slowly, the plan matured in him. Decisions can come too early or too late, but they almost never come "just in time." Downing twenty tablets, was that enough? That was enough, he considered. And it should be enough. His watch struck seven. Carefully, he slipped out of bed and pulled on some shorts and a shirt. He left the room barefoot. He tiptoed up the inside stairs to the restaurant. He ordered breakfast for two, a pot of coffee, and two full glasses of yogurt. Fifteen minutes later, he came down the stairs with a full tray. In the bathroom, he continued on as silent as a blade to the edge of the bathtub. He crept into the bedroom. Aisha was in the same position as he had left her having the same cheerful smile on her shapely lips. What was she dreaming of? He took the two boxes of Vesparax and crept back to the bathroom. On the sheet, he slid the glass yogurt forward.

"Twenty tablets are enough for everyone," he muttered, giving himself courage.

Then, he hesitated a moment. What right do I have about her life? But if I only renounce them, they will be left with the pieces in a foreign country in a suspicious light. I can't do that to her. Resolutely, he opened one of the boxes and shook the contents into a palm. He stared aghast at the strip. Nervously, he opened the second box. All the strips were empty. Almost mechanically, he turned to the door of the bathroom and threw an uncertain glance toward the slumbering Aisha, fresh as the morning. Then, his flashed gaze to where the boxes were located.

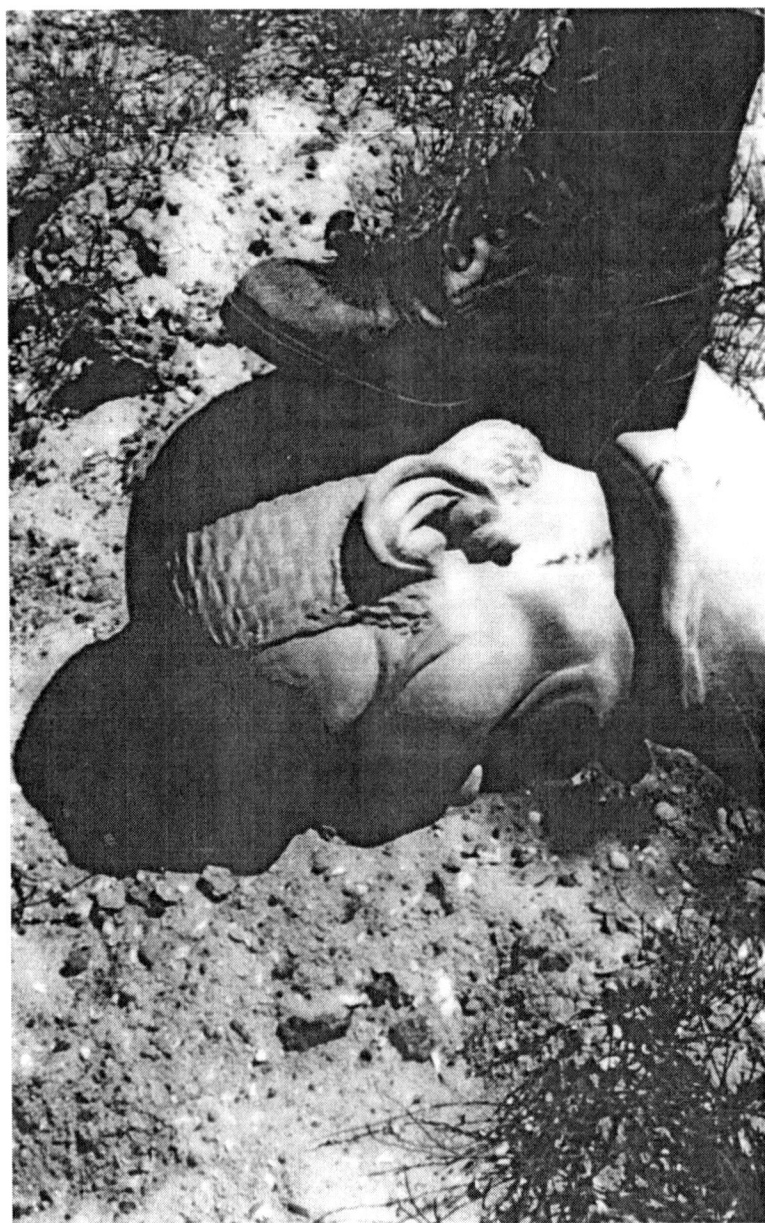

ONE OF THEM

The unidentified man tier.
Helmuth Plessner

It began in the fall began. Yes, that sounds about right. Right in the beginning of early autumn. It was nearing August, or it was mid-July. It seemed like it was in the air. Its thin mists can't be dislodged. It was almost palpable. It was in the atmosphere. Was it an indefinable feeling? Of course, feelings are deceptive. In any case, something seemed to have changed that would originally have remained the same. But what? Was it perhaps the new government?

Gradually, petty crime was taken off the streets. Or was that how it seemed? Maybe it was harshly done. In any case, no fuss was made about it, nor of the hard crime that was dealt with a heavy hand. Things weren't fixed either way. Anyway, the missteps of the greats of the past were included. There was no mention of it in the press. Were they suppressed by the law to protect against the little ones so that they would not be small and victimized by short-sightedness? So it goes. The large hand gives out the sheets in smaller napkins. The bottom layer should be satisfied with paper towels, if it's lucky. Toilet paper. Cheap quality.

Sport. The newspapers were full of the sport like never before. Maybe the system thought to give the people bread and circuses. Of course, what should you put the people in besides hunger and war? Well, a new order will appear progressively and everything should be done a little different. The ordering believed in matter. The spirit, or something of that nature, already had enough. It was felt. In the newspapers and on radio and television, much attention was paid to the review of concerts and serious music. Or what one might know below.

Preference was given to "something unique." What was that exactly? Lessons will follow. There were courses even for folklore and dances. Old hats, but still...

Contemporary art came off badly. It was never flawlessly received. That means courage. It's hard to get used to the unknown. At the expense of the well-known, they don't want their judgment. This one should be born again. At the theater, the offers were strictly watched. Cabaret was the stepchild. Okay, cabaret was originally suffering from being prostituted. Rural suffering was banished, as was claimed. Does that also mean less laughter? Now that we think about it, it was decided less laughter. Was there no reason to smile? There's enough reason to smile. Yet, there was little laughter in public. You traitor never sleeps. Traitors? No one knew for sure. Suspicions were everywhere. It would better if they're not heard. Now and then, a person disappeared. Maybe due to the marriage cases. My girlfriend's in another place, in another country, or something.

The streetscape. The street's been retrenched. It's probably because of the transition from the grinning summer to the dreary, chilly autumn. As I said, it's mid-July to early August.

The jeans came into vogue. You could hardly wear anything more. Jeans, a black T -shirt under a gray / blue jacket, and a gray cap. Even clerks wear it. The police also ran in jeans. They had a dark blue jacket on with brass buttons and they sported a blue service cap with black flap. A leading major newspaper wrote a critical article: "Jeans Culture." The next day, the editors put out a rectification. All this was based on a misunderstanding, they said. In the next edition, they offered their apologies to the readers. The reporter had been fired. Rightly so, one should not want to patronize the preference of the people. "The voice of the people is the voice of God." Homer wrote in a fixed newspaper column.

There was a lot of smoke. Yet, cigarettes were financially promoted as a mainstay for healthcare and thus have become increasingly expensive. And there were more drunkards than ever. They claimed that it was all in moderation although that wasn't fully established. Or was there a need to combat the chill, a more need for inner warmth?

The fashion changes with the season and the seasons change with the fashion; the joke of a careless prankster. The madness of today is tomorrow's fashion and vice versa.

Mr. Harrie (Herbert) Kosnic, a man with an unobtrusive appearance in his late thirties, dressed modestly. He was the principal administrator of a reputable central purchasing food. Blablabla blablabla.

Around mid-September, he was summoned by the management. Was there going to be a change in management? He knew that none of the trio received him in jeans and gray jackets. He noticed that all three of them had cut their hair bristly short. Was that the new trend? Under new management, under new trends.

"Mr. Kosnic," the middle of the men, whose appearance was dominated by a black-edged glasses, addressed him, "you said in an interview with one or more employees" - he glanced at the writing – "a good servant hates his master. Is that right?"

Mr. Kosnic searched his memory for piles of unwanted lies and several layers of whole and half-truths. Before he could bring say something, the man took a second look at the papers:

"That's not all. It says here that you intoned, "Behind every capital is a villainy!" He looked at the other attentively through his portholes as if he was an exotic insect. He paused to measure an effect. "For this reason, we are compelled to dismiss you."

Mr. Kosnic's color changed.

"I could not have said that," he protested shakily, "Maybe someone has taken my words out of context."

"You hinted that in a conversation with colleagues," came the castrate voice of the rightmost man among the trio. He was a fat man with a chin that started near the collarbone up. He had a mouth that that looked like the slit of a piggy bank and he had kakwangen near the bags under his eyes.

"Spiritual pollution," croaked the third, a gaunt figure with steel blue eyes. His carefully trimmed mustache revealed a cold grin. "You can't deny this."

He raised his chin defiantly forward with a sour expression, as if has just suckled some vinegar. A bad comparison, Mr. Kosnic considered. Persuasion is no argument here.

"There is no comment that can't be fitted with corrective comments." Mr. Kosnic said.

The trio didn't wish this to happen.

"Even the thought is suspect, in your position you should have known that strict confidentiality of mind is a code of honor."

"It may be that I quoted something, or in general have put something forward. But what you have is not concrete. I believe in a book… I can't remember the name of the book. I'm prevented in paraphrasing it. But it came during a break in the talks, and Proudhon was the author. I think... It could also have been Max Stirner."

"An excuse," the potbelly man sneered triumphantly who saw analyzed this as a confession. Perhaps he had never heard of Proudhon or Stirner. Who could blame him?

Is it possible to survive without excuses? Mr. Kosnic considered. He sought without success with convincing arguments. His mind was acutely paralyzed. He can't recall what needs to be remembered. His thoughts and intentions were thwarted by the unexpected resignation that he noticed from his three executioners.

"That's enough," the first spokesman noted, "for someone with such a reading, is accountable suspect. And then also ventilate in company! It should be clear that we can't tolerate this."

Mr. Kosnic was silent. People who are so antagonistic usually can't be persuaded to go towards a different direction. He accused his mind in a flash of brightness.

"The cashier will, despite the fact that barely a half month's passed, pay you a whole month's salary which includes your holiday," said the owl with a happy expression. "You can go."

Arrogance of power, Mr. Kosnic noted. He did not want to go. He wanted to protest against his dismissal. He disappeared without hearing a word from them through a side door. Mr. Kosnuc felt like a beaten dog.

The dismissal made Harry Kosnic come home from work earlier than usual that afternoon. Emilie, his wife who was five years younger than him, was running errands. Timidly, he took off his suit and changed to his house clothes. He sat on a bench and pondered his situation. Fifteen years of loyal service and in just one moment he was kicked out in the street. How do you get a job when you're almost forty? Young forces are preferred. They do the same work, do more, and are paid less. But come, I must not become dejected. Emilie's summer suffered from the recent loss of her mother. Emilie was originally a victim of religion. Through her marriage to Harry Kosnic, she was there almost cured. Because of family ties, she periodically suffered from religious regurgitations. Emilie and Harrie Kosnic had what was generally called a good marriage. That is, they applied themselves down to the facts. In their life force, they nurtured their relationship with every opportunities that arose. They suffered from a regular and fairly dull life. This kind of life consisted largely of their inaccessibility with each other, as was common in the average person. Although they suffered no disastrous consequences so far. Besides, Harry Kosnic wouldn't want things to be different. He heard a key turning the lock. Emilie entered with a bag full of groceries. When she saw her husband sitting in the room, she was surprised and stood for a moment in silence.

"You're early," she said.

Harry nodded gloomily. His gaze wandered off. "How do I tell my wife without creating a drama? Let me take the facts. What do I know? In fact, I actually know nothing. The question is whether or not these facts exist. Or do they exist solely in the moods we experience? They usually become fiction afterwards. The difference between fact and fiction is that there's a very shadowy area on the border of probability and fantasy. Harry decided to come out with the truth. "Yes, I'm early." He sighed. "I've been fired." The high word was out.

Frightened, Emilie dropped the shopping bag. A packaged of bread rolled on the floor as if it was also shocked. Harry gave an account of what had happened that afternoon.

"Almost fifteen years of being punctual every day. I was never ill. There was one exception but that was when I was really sick. For fifteen years I've faithfully done my duty! In the last five years I've been chief administrator and now..." He finished his sentence flatly. He thought Emilie was about to burst in tears. Harry looked at her to comfort her. She was inconsolable, he knew. Her feelings were so fragile. The reality of this moment was loaded with something that hurt him. What exactly did he grasp in his difficult thoughts? Let alone in his words? It was probably the banality of her reaction. What could he expect? Emilie had a limited horizon in her small universe. She could often look at him if she did not know the way. In tears, they deposited the groceries in the kitchen cupboards.

"Can't we on vacation?" she sang her elegy.

"I'm devastated that the dismissal happened during the holidays," Harry snorted. His nature of reality has been violated. Their last vacation in early spring came back to him. The past is past but the spirit lives on. Now, it seemed to him that the past was an orgy of well-being in anticipation of the final disaster. Prosperity contributes to impoverishment of morality.

Especially when the Big One makes the business up. All has been going well in the company where he worked. Last year, he was rewarded for his efforts during the computerization. And now...

Harrie Kosnic was back to square one in his career, with his thoughts, and with his Emilie. Let us not despair, he comforted himself. Hope or despair both come from the same strain and structure. In the sea of hope, one can be overwhelmed by a tidal wave of despair. Emilie prepared the food. He glanced at the newspaper looking for a job. An hour later, they were sitting at the table. During the meal, they ate in silence. Tears welled in her eyes and one rolled down her nose. What can tears do at a time like this? Harry thought compassionately. He thought the food was bland. We have the consolation of laughter and a small changes here and there. Yet, there was nothing to laugh about. After dinner, he did the dishes as usual and then made coffee. Coffee would offer some consolation for the day!

"Why did you have to say?" Emilie bleated.

"What?"

"From the servant and master. You have your mouth beyond talking. Don't deny it."

Now, the blame. Harry paused and put the cups on a tray. Any clarification would increase the veil of misunderstanding. Moreover, he knew her desertion from the rational world all too well. Emilie wanted her equal. She feels unhappy when things aren't done right. That is its weak link, and ergo also mine. Habitually, he pulled her closer by her left shoulder as she began her sermon. During the half-hour coffee session, he endured an avalanche of accusations about himself. When the nagging bored him and after he has had a second cup, he ostentatiously turned on their old TV set.

"Ah," he said during a break in her tirade. His mood has improved inexplicably, "I'll find a job here or there. What does not seem possible should be possible."

After the news, a politician on the world stage said he was in favor of their own parish because he had nothing to report. Then debit past the new president, coupe à la brittle, with a bulging pouch improbabilities "our enemies." To whom that hit was not entirely clear. Whoever rules will use the power of truth or put truth in a suspicious light and claim the results equal from the outset.

As usual, midnight came and the scene which, as usual, pretended to be "true" came on. "It puts too much focus on faith to get credibility," Harry thought. "Truth" is elevated to a surrogacy of nonsense. Man is a trivial mistake of nature. I made the mistake of allowing my birth partly because I could not avoid it. That will avenge me someday. If you keep at it, nothing good will ever come out of it.

Meanwhile, Emilie wore a lachrymose face that night. Harry provisionally could not sleep. He waited until he heard her coming to bed and he switched to a pornographic foreign channel. After an hour, he capitulated to the total dominance of the TV and zapped an orgy. The battle remained undecided. Exhausted by the struggle, he retired about two hours from the unit. "Gay sapiens," he thought and put on his pajamas. He went to the bathroom and brushed his teeth. Then, he visited the toilet as usual. He pushed gently at Emilie between the sheets without waking her. Tonight, there would be no adult entertainment. Those were his last thoughts.

A month passed. Their life has daily become frugal compared to their previous lifestyle. Harrie Kosnic found, after five weeks, work at a large factory of sugar products. Compared to his previous job, his was a meager office job which earned slightly more than half of his former income.

In order not to fall out of place, he has been wearing jeans, a gray jacket with cap, and a bristly hairdo. The office was tucked away on the fifth attic of a large factory building. From the beginning, he did not feel at home there. But that was also true to the common home, he consoled himself. He sat at a desk in front of a closet with thick folders full of alphabetical correspondence. Regularly, he took letters from other clerks which they needed for their work. After using, such letters were often misplaced in the files. Kosnic's task was to check whether or not all the letters were arranged in alphabetical order, dated, and that all errors have been corrected. He started with the letter A. And, after more than a week, he was at the end of Z. Then, he started with letter A again. During the second round, he decided to store the returned letters. Important errors took less time. His chief regarded the new clerk after three weeks as a useful work force. One night about half past five, the factory siren mooed for the second time. The staff left the factory as usual. Just before his departure, Kosnic needed to use the toilet. The lavatory for the office staff appeared was being cleaned by the cleaning service. Why so soon? He decided to seek the toilet in the next floor. Maybe it was still open. After he had reached the stairs, he passed a fence that wasn't shut down. But he did not know that. The sounds he heard came over his head during the office hours. It made him curious as to what took place there in the attic. Before he entered the toilet, he cast a searching look around the corner. It turned out to be a large room full of unknown plant equipment. There were a few workers around.

When Kosnic was done, almost everyone had left. Suddenly, the lights were turned off. He was in the middle of the attic. Only a single neon tube burned. In the near darkness, he ran the wrong way and could not find the stairs down. After some searching among unfamiliar equipment, he finally ended up in a lift on the other side of the building. It was currently being boarded by a number of workers. A couple of guards happened to pass the office. They wore the same clothes as the city police and they were armed with a revolver and a rubber truncheon. In their belt, an unknown device hung. Kosnic paid no further attention to them and stepped into the elevator. The doors closed and the elevator dropped. Everyone looked silently at himself. On the ground floor, the elevator stopped and the doors slid open on the other side. There appeared a short scantily lit corridor. There was a sofa on both sides. Everyone sat down. It was agreed that only the two guards stood. Kosnic hesitated. What was he doing here? Was this the ground floor? Strange.

"Have you the twelve, colleague?" a voice sounded through an intercom.

"Okay," one of the guards replied.

Behind his back, the doors closed. The corridor began to tremble. Kosnic, who had also stopped, stared and wondered what this could all mean. He noted that they were moving. The short way they took after they got off the lift was actually the cargo hold of a car. He wanted to ask the guard. Without a word, he was pushed on a couch. The man made a gesture with his rubber baton and shook his head. Kosnic started to protest but thought better of it. He'd naturally find out that it was a mistake, he supposed. The sounds penetrated from the outside. To Kosnic, it was clear that they were traffic sounds. After ten minutes. The car stopped. A short pause was followed by going back and forth before the doors opened. Another corridor and this time it was long. Four guards were waiting for them. The only difference with the previous guards was that they kept their foreign device in their hands. The device blinked with a red light and it had some sort of Geiger counter. Not a word was exchanged. Kosnic concluded that his presence here was based on a misunderstanding. He was rudely pushed in line. They had to go through the corridor towards a door with bars. Suddenly, one of the guards exclaimed:

"Doernin isn't here!"

"I still have the twelve," a guard reported, surprised.

"Yeah, I get it. Doernin has escaped! This is a new one. He does not chip and it's obvious that a substitute helped him."

Kosnic was brusquely pushed forward.

"Hell, he does not have the chip."

"Of course. One of the gang members sacrificed himself."

Kosnic, who still did not understand, was conducted by the two guards to a room that had a desk and a few chairs. He wondered if he was dreaming or if he has just landed in a grim tale. The reality, though it was a vague concept, was palpable. A guard behind the desk invited him to sit down with a gesture of his hand. Then, he began his interrogation. Kosnic told his simple story. A second guard entered. And a third guard. They all asked him the same questions while the other two verified their notes.

"We don't believe a single damn, Kosnic. Confess that you're an accomplice of Doernin. Then, we will see what we can do for you to reduce your punishment in helping the enemy," the last questioner promised.

"I have nothing to confess except all that I've told. I don't know this Doering fellow or whatever you call that man."

"Okay, then you don't get to go. You're forcing us to apply tougher measures, suspect Kosnic." The man pressed a bell. Three other guards appeared and seized him by the arms. He was then dragged to a cell. They beat him with their rubber batons, batons called langelat. Soon, Kosnic lost consciousness. A bucket of water was splashed on him to revive him.

"Do you know who Doernin is?" the guards shouted in his ear. He shook his head. The guards beat him again and he forgot that he even existed. When Kosnic opened his eyes again, he made an effort to think. He felt heavily damaged. He felt as if he was beaten in two separate parts. He tried to take a slightly different approach. He groped around. The loft where they had imprisoned him was hardly a square meter. Every movement caused him pain. He was bleeding from his several wounds. His mouth and throat felt like sandpaper. His eyes were swollen and he had lost a few teeth. He was tormented by an unbearable thirst. He was exhausted. He fell into a state of apathy. The slightest noise startled him. Time passed. Soon, he couldn't even remember how long he lay there. He had lost consciousness several times. Suddenly, a door opened and the room was illuminated. He was dragged into a room and he was questioned again. He could only respond vaguely. He kept on denying that he was an accomplice of Doernin by shaking his head. Why was he so stubborn amidst this layer of mystery? A false confession would have been easier. Harrie Kosnic proved to be stubborn and unyielding.

"He's a tough guy, but we can get it out of him," a voice sounded somewhere in the background.

They put him under a cold shower and rocked him again with their bats. In any case, the cold helped. His wounds began to bleed. Kosnic came to a vague consciousness when someone yelled in his ear:

"Confess now, asshole."

He was capable of doing nothing. A foggy thought occurred to him: hero. This was another word for stupidity. He has passed the stage of being a coward or a hero. He was put on a chair. He was too weak to remain sitting upright and his posture slumped. Waves of unconsciousness swept over him. Yet, his mind and body remained unyielding. It refused to budge. Though he was helpless, they grabbed his hand and made him scribble something on a piece of paper. Then, the executioners dragged him by the arms to a cell. There were five other inmates in that cell. They laid him on a bottom bunk and whispered something in his ear. His mind was too far away to understand anything. They tried to make him drink some water. The water spilled as they poured it between his teeth. He swallowed hard and lost all consciousness again.

The next morning, his world remained the same. One of the cellmates shook him silently by the shoulder and fed him his breakfast: hard sour bread and a cup of weak tea. Kosnic wanted to eat something but he did not succeed. His other cellmates supported him and he slobbered small sips of tea. In the late afternoon, he ate some cabbage stew. "I can't eat," he thought, "nor can I think." His limbs seemed broken. His wounds burned, and his teeth chattered from the fever. It took over a week before Harry Kosnic managed to achieve a more stable level of consciousness. He wanted to thank his fellow prisoners for their good care.

"Don't mention it," whispered a cellmate, "We all know the happiness in getting to move without pain."

They whispered to him that he had to say as little as possible. The walls and ceiling were bugged. Whenever the cellmates wanted to speak to each other, they did so with a breath to the ear.

"I have nothing to hide," Kosnic weakly claimed, "I really have nothing to hide. I'm innocent."

One of the others put a hand on his mouth and hissed:

"We all are. But that's not the point."

"The punishment, whether or not it's true, is to bring your guilt to light," whispered a second. Kosnic nodded slightly as if he understood.

"The guards are guilty rats."

"An affront to the rat people."

"Anyone who ends up behind bars don't escape. We are all guilty. We must trust in God," said a third cellmate.

"God? God is a stumbling representation of ourselves. Every man creates his own God and clings to it. To drown you in life, like us. Death is the only option."

"We are the misfits of a failed man."

"All the misery of the world is placed in a pile and then distributed to humans."

"One day, God will allow his dog to fart a big turd. God kneaded a globe and threw it in the gutter. After six days, man came out from the sludge pile."

"Spotters get spotters' wage. You are blasphemers."

"Stop it," a cellmate said with a dismissal arm, "God tolerates everything."

"Despite the fact that you spit on Him?"

"We spit on him! God is no better than the rest. He's a bad man as much as He is a criminal."

Thus the sober whispered conversation between the cellmates went. Harrie Kosnic remained silent. The conversation was barely useful. Insofar, what they nonsense they said made sense. Their conversations consisted of sniffer's language, or some information of dubious nature which leads to deformation. There was meaning in the meaninglessness. Thoughts? It was from one blend to the other. Are you long for somewhere doing, then it will tend to instinctively want to pursue a purpose. Mind you they unfortunately don't submit it to the chain. But still, Kosnic remembered a counsel by a former teacher in mind: "Keep your mind open but don't lose your mind. The spirit in which we are dressed in is as moth-eaten as a shabby Dalles biplane."

After the fourteenth day, Kosnic Harrie recovered little. He felt extremely weak. Like his cellmates, he relied on the minimum pleasures of life. In this case, two meager meals a day. A few times a day he followed his cellmates' conversation. He participated in his silence.

"You are silent, and you only nod. Why don't you share something about yourself?"

"I've always been a zwijgertje. My view holds matters little." He recalled the events of two months ago. "Once you open your mouth, you'll get in trouble." The other cellmates nodded at his words and thought about his words, whatever they be.

In a short time, one of the cell mates was moved and replaced by another. The newcomer aroused suspicion.

"A provocateur," breathed a companion in Kosnic's ear. He felt the newcomer was trying to win their trust. None of the old cellmates responded. Their insolence can't be so large, an insolence the opposition called imperturbability. They occasionally exchanged a word or two. The inmates hid in their own thoughts and adapted to the situation. What else could they do? Silently, they walked up and down the cell layers with their hands under the head of their crib.

After a week, the provocateur disappeared. That same day, a badly beaten newcomer was delivered. Just as Kosnic had recently, the newcomer was welcomed in the circle and cared for. Involuntarily, they created the band. The whispered conversations resumed. Sometimes, someone was removed from the cell and did not return. There were two possibilities: the man was transferred to another cell or he was tortured to death. The next day, another victim was thrown by the guards.

A week later, it was Kosnic's turn. He was led to an unknown destination and he hoped for the best. A guard took him to the same small room where he had recently been. On the wall behind the desk hung a medicine cabinet. The guard stood at the door and told him that he had to sit in the chair and he waved demonstratively with his langelat. A few moments later, a man in a white coat came inside. On his broad shoulders danced a narrow head with square jaws. The cubic skull was equipped with gray hair and deep-set eyes. The impression Kosnic had was the transparency between the eternity of the past and the future. The appearance basically has nothing to do with it. It can accommodate a human or a monster. I fear the latter.

The man, who was apparently a doctor, have him a glance. He sat behind the desk and looked bored on a list that he pulled out of a drawer.

"Your name," he squeezed the words out of his thin lips without looking up. As if every word he said was too much, Kosnic thought silently. He was so naive to believe that this was a place for politeness. The man looked past him as if his sight was contagious.

"If you don't want to say it, you lose the right to speak."

The then doctor nodded to the guard who took a step forward and nudged his elbow between Kosnic's ribs. "I guess you realize that clobbering me is futile?" Kosnic wondered.

"My name is Herbert Kosnic... sir," he emphasized the last word. He failed to make a single impression.

"You'll have get a chip inserted, Kosnic. You'll shortly become a chipmunk. If you are released, and should that ever happen, we will neutralize the chip. Bare your upper body bare."

Kosnic did as he was told. The doctor rose to his feet, picked up a few things from the medicine cabinet, and laid it on the desk. He walked around the desk and gave Kosnic an anesthetic with a lancet before creating a deep incision in his left upper arm near the shoulder. Then, he pressed a small capsule in the wound. He sewed the skin close with a wound closer. It was a painful procedure, but Kosnic did not budge. "You must have studied gorilla medicine, your moral degenerate," he thought. The doctor wiped the blood off with a piece of paper from a paper towel. He sprayed a styptic haze over the wound.

"After a week, you can scratch off that layer Kosnic. Surgically, the capsule can't be removed. If you ever derive this arm with blood, in twenty-four hours, the capsule will crack open and release poison." The doctor nodded again to the guard. Kosnic's arm remained painful. He was then transported to an isolation cell.

For a week, he remained trapped in this little cell. He missed his companions. Their company was better than none although that wasn't always the case.

He was awakened early in the morning. For the first time, he had to appear flush with five unknown munks on apple. Then, they were returned to an empty cell. The munks took him with suspicion. He understood their attitude, rolled his sleeve, and showed the wound. Someone silently nodded and he got the impression that he was accepted. The usual breakfast was pushed in through the hatch. After half an hour, the cell door opened and the group was led to a bus. There were six of them. The van drove the munks away.

The destination turned out to be the same factory where Kosnic, was appointed as an office clerk not so long ago. The elevator aligned with the bus and took the chipmunks to the sixth attic. Under the supervision of a group of guards, they were put to work in the Hard Bales department. They had to empty their pockets before they got in the warehouse which was located at street level. There were led by a to a drudgery. A piston sucked the pulp that was processed on the seventh attic by other munks and they purified molasses. On the eighth attic, a metal torpedo was poured in shapes of sugar loaves. After they cooled, the loaves were milled off at the bottom at the right weight. Then, the loaves went to the ninth attic where other munks wrapped them in blue paper. Through a narrow paternoster, there were cups that could contain eight loaves. They were then dropped to manufacture parterre. From there they were packed in boxes and exported abroad.

Fifteen of them were brought at that time. They quickly had to gobble a meal inside. There were about fifteen groups of six chipmunks running the place. That morning at seven o'clock, the buses delivered twelve chipmunks off at the factory. Between six and seven o'clock in the evening, the munks were driven back to prison. They had only an hour's rest per day, and they worked five days a week from morning at nine o'clock until they've worked five hours. The place was ran by munks seven days a week. This work gave them an advantage. Instead of eating twice like the other prisoners, they were given a sober meal three times a day. Kosnic was not used to physical labor. Due to the many beatings, he was emaciated and weakened. The first few weeks, he was broken on the wheel. Once they were back in the cell, he threw himself on his bed, exhausted. It took a month before his muscles evolved. The guards in the attics of carried a revolver and small device was called the chipklikker. Once this the device has been activated, the munk's chip from a distance of eight meters would start to flicker.

Harrie Kosnic had all the time to consider his situation. Escaping was practically nil. There were some who managed to escape, like Doernin. Of course, he wasn't alone. There were some men who cooperated and he bribed some guards. Usually, a fugitive was caught within a few days and shot on the spot or thrown half dead thrown into a cell. Since, the guards thrashed him until he died. To save his life, to the extent that there was in him, all known what she wanted from him and forced to sign. Police and security solved these issues in concert. A corrupt judge in a certain administrative position would ensure punishment of three to six months' solitary confinement in a damp loft. If the victim survived even that, he was employed elsewhere again, a probate method to breed slaves as cheap labor.

The reign of terror stopped at nothing. He led his life in silent protest. How should you give meaning to futility? Life is cynical. He could not get used to the stultifying work. At that time, he worked like a robot. But in the evening after work and at weekends, he could roll a stone from the mountain and he was free to relax and do what he wanted to. To that extent, that you did not run the system for the feet, as was proved. Or was that freedom curtailed? Freedom was most appreciated in places where it doesn't exist. Spiritually, we are free. The power of the spirit can stand against the spirit of power! There is something to do and they can move freely. Freedom means the right to think differently, to live, and let live.

As long as you don't offend anyone or discriminate anyone, it's freedom. That one may be of utter impunity but without it there would be consequences. On one of those days, he heard a fellow prisoner hiss while passing the toilet in his ear:

"Doernin, the chef, knows he has his freedom thanks to you. He is counting on you."

Kosnic nodded and wondered who this Doernin could be. The chef? What did that mean? That evening, he talked to Barwitz, a cellmate, who has long been a slave of the work.

After some whispering, he discovered that Doernin was the leader of a resistance group. Was he the opposition to the system? How would that work? What was the reason why Doernin was counting on him? Barwitz knew nothing. Or pretended to know nothing. A short time later, he asked Kosnic if it was possible to attempt an escape.

"I don't know," growled Kosnic evasively. Was this man be trusted? One should not heroïseren himself. The first instance has to be considered. It can cost lives. But cowardice enables the price. The situation he was in was slavery at a much better course. Opposing would bring about terrible risks. Risks? So was that what his life was about! He asked Barwitz who the man was, and if he could send Doernin a message. He confided that his name was Katovic. It turned out that some time ago, he himself tried to escape. His arrest brought him to the brink of death. That was enough information for Kosnic to let himself be convinced of Katovic's integrity. After some whispered consultation with his cellmates, he decided to risk participating in the uprising that was brought about with it.

Six cells were involved. They knew each other and more or less supported each other. To avoid treachery, the group of conspirators was kept small. Doernin, the mastermind behind the scenes, had drawn up a plan. It was pretty simple. Initially, the group of guards in the attic needed to be overpowered and disarmed. The munks would then seek refuge through the elevators and stairs if that was possible. It was speculated on that the munks of the remaining cells would join them immediately. The basic group would leave the unit of the factory. On the large car park next to the factory, they could count on help from like-minded people for the necessary transportation. For an individual insurgent, that would mean that every man was for himself, and that God was against all the ordering. A group was also organized to take the higher attic.

The uprising was scheduled on a Sunday afternoon half an hour after the change of guard at half past six that day. On the lower attics were offices, laboratories, and warehouses. The garage didn't work on weekends. The munks counted on meeting moderate resistance so they could force a way out. Doernin each assigned a special task to them. Kosnic had made Barwitz the guardian of the toilet on his behalf.

The toilet was near the open entrance to the link beside four basins and across four booths. Each booth was equipped with the famous hurk. It was either a Turkish toilet or a hole in the stone floor between two footrests. The height of the squat toilet was about four feet and was a foot above the floor. The open spaces above and below the doors were patrolled by guards. They regularly checked the boxes and toilets if they were occupied, who is using them, and if there was anything else going on.

That Sunday, with the support of the munks, they waited until it was eight o'clock in the evening. Nothing indicated that irregularities could occur. In the cells of the base, all actions must be done accurately. Someone with an eye for detail would have noticed that in the recent weeks, the cells whispered more than usual. A good half hour later, the munks found their redemption at the agreed strategic points. Katovic, the leader of the rebellion, gave the signal by blowing his nose.

Kosnic went to the toilet and crouched behind the door of one of the booths. He waited anxiously for Barwitz to come a moment later and occupy the box. Soon, a guard appeared.

"What the hell!? Look at this!" Kosnic cried.

With his hands out of sight, the guard approached and threw a condescending look at the door. Kosnic grabbed him under the door at his trouser legs. Barwitz flew out the other box out and hit the guard. The guard could not get away. They pounded at his head with the heel of a shoe. The guard then collapsed. Kosnic, who quickly left his booth, grabbed the bat out of his hand and gave him an additional blow to the head. Barwitz grabbed the revolver. He had fewer scruples than Kosnic. The groggy guard was pressed down. Then, he tore the chipklikker off his belt. Barwitz hastily put his shoe back on while Kosnic dragged the guard's heavy corpse to a toilet booth. Then, they both threw themselves into the fray at the workplace where a battle with hooks and bats raged. The monitoring was insufficiently prepared. A rebellion never happened before. They used their langelat and dared not to use their firearms in fear that they would hit a colleague in the fight. Barwitz wielded his weapon and, with the nonchalance of a god, ousted two guards at sight. With a few exceptions, other munks had joined the rebels when they understood that this was their chance. The doubters were the first to use the chaos to seek refuge through a fire escape. Two chipmunks were killed in the battle. Also, on the upper attics, another battle was fought. The government had not taken account of a general uprising. Soon, there were no more guard in the attics. The hatred of the munks was so great that she guards, who had surrendered, were flung out the windows with their own weapons. A chipmunk wrestled with a guard and he bit the guard's larynx open. There was still blood in his stubble. A guard had succeeded with a walkie-talkie alarm to save some time for his brain were smashed. Somewhere outside, a siren began to wail. The rebels ran to the elevators. No more than fifteen men could be in the elevator at once. The rest thundered down the stairs. On the second attic, they were met by a group of guards with drawn revolvers. Shots were fired and victims fell. Some unarmed munks wore a bale of pulp to protect for the body. A small group of rebels were driven back. The guards wanted to come up the stairs but they were pelted with bales of pulp and the staircase threatened to collapse. Part of the Doerningroep descended to one of the lifts. The enemy attacked the stairwell at the back. The anger of the munks were insatiable. The fight had to be settled here pretty quickly. Three guards surrendered. They were disarmed and liquidated on the spot. Other cell groups rushed out. Others scattered throughout the factory and sought refuge and reached via the fire stairs at the back of the factory building. From a window on the first loft, a group of refugees came out. A guard who was holed up opened fire. Two munks turned their weapons on the shooter and they hit him in the head.

On the broad quay, where a month ago loads of sugar had been unloaded, Kosnic breathed deep and hard. But what now? He saw more individual fighting than he had originally intended. He thought that the group would be too big of a target. Any straggler from the guards would be shot on sight. The Doerningroep, a thirty man group, ran across a parking lot on the side of the factory building and disappeared by a gate. The munks not belonging to the resistance proliferated. Indecisive, Kosnic ran at a random direction. The siren still wailed. There, at the head of the wharf, he could see police van driving to the factory complex. From the opposite side, guards approached a group near a large machine shop. The insurgents who knew the area had left the factory building at the rear. The refugees who were on the quay were embedded. Kosnic was one of the first who dove into the water of the canal. The rest followed. It was freezing, but it hardly bother him now since his life was at stake. On the way to the other side of the wide channel, he lost the bat in his waistband. The guards were already at a considerable distance. They opened fire at the swimmers from the factory quay. A chipmunk was hit and drowned. Another chipmunk who could not swim and dared not cross wanted to return to the plant and find another way out. He was simply shot. Kosnic swam under water as much as possible. On the other side, the refugees helped each other on shore under a hail of bullets. No one was hit. The distance was too great and it was getting darker. A group of refugees spread all around and each of them sought refuge. Kosnic ran with a few others along the railroad tracks. After more than a kilometer, they reached the dilapidated shed of an old shipyard.

Kosnic was out of breath. He felt his side stabbing with pain and had to rest. The rest ran by. He was sorry that he had not been at the Doerningroep. He decided in to break the rickety doors off their hinges. Inside, he found shelter. He found a basement and removed the metal sheet of a rusty door. It was locked on the outside. Panting from exertion, he sank down on a crate. After a short time, his breathing restored. He decided to stay here because it would soon be dark. There was barely any light outside. He saw was a collection of rusty machinery and packaging waste inside. The basement had no second exit. "I must keep this in mind," he realized. His teeth chattering, he took off his meager togs and wrung the water out. He also did some stationary exercises which made his temperature drop. Once he stopped the exercises, the cold took possession of him again. There was enough wood crates and cardboard to light a fire. But where would he get the matches? With chattering teeth, he went to explored the dark shed as quietly as possible. Somewhere in the middle of the room was a gas, a rusty sink, and crushed plastic cups and other rubbish. He had nothing to complain about. With a hand, he poked into one of the hills of dust. He found a flattened matchbox and a nearly empty lighter. Between the burnt matches he found three unused ones. Kosnic hurried back to the basement and made a bonfire of cardboard and wood crates. He decided to spend the night here. He clutched some cardboard and a rope end to the inside of the door to the basement. He capped the window with an old piece of tarpaulin. The dry wood made very little smoke and after a short time, the temperature became bearable.

Early in the morning of the next day, his clothes were already quite dry. Kosnic went again to search in the canteen. He hoped he'd find something to his liking. He unexpectedly heard a car stop and the sound of voices. A door was closed and footsteps approached. He peered around a corner of the canteen. Two young officers entered. Their guns were drawn.

"Looking costs nothing. It would not surprise me if a few of those guys are lurking here," someone said softly.

"Yeah. And they're waiting for us!"

"You never know." The first speaker snorted. "Do you smell something?" The other snorted.

"Hell, a burning smell."

"It's coming from that side. If they are still there, we have a surprise in store for them."

"Maybe you're right. Careful, they have weapons and... " the conversation continued in whispers.

Revolver in one hand, flashlight in the other, they fell on their toes down the stairs to the basement where the fire came.

"There's smoke," whispered one of the agents.

"Beware. There's a fire smoldering there. "

"Police! Hands high," roared the bravest of the two. He pulled the door wide open, gun at the ready.

"Nothing." They entered the basement and went to investigate.

"Careful. You never know now," repeated agent number one.

"I told you that they saw us coming."

If they ever search this place, then I'm screwed, the thought flashed through Kosnic's mind. Death is a privilege in bad weather. But this was no time for fear and trembling. He talked himself to courage. It was all or nothing. He crept almost silently towards the basement stairs. If he went down the stairs, that would make noise and take too much time. He crouched and jumped off the side eight feet down. With one blow, he slammed the door and crouched. His assailants, who were inspecting the basement, became surprised. Because of the obstacles that stood everywhere, they arrived too late at the exit. Kosnic was already at the top of the stairs. He emptied his lungs to discharge the tension. The officers fired blank shots at the iron door. He ran the length of the great hall. At the exit, he saw a lot of cobble that had served as a ballast from the past. A boulder is a suitable weapon in this time of need, he considered. He lit a match that he stored in his pocket. The two losers in the basement kept ramming on the iron door. Outside, the engine of the car hummed. Kosnic stepped in and drove back along the railroad tracks and sheds. It was Monday morning. There were workers biking to work. He saw a police car and an ambulance standing across the wide channel of the sugar factory. "I shouldn't be too fond of this," he thought, and he drove on before he roused their suspicion. His gaze slid towards the glove compartment where there were some papers and handcuffs layers. On an impulse, he threw everything out of a side window on the verge. Can he remain anonymous in the downtown area? Or were there policemen with chip clickers around?

On the border of the low-rise industrial and residential area was a junkyard and a few other small businesses. Here, everything was closed and nobody was in sight. Kosnic put the car between two scrapped cars and parked in front of the gate. With his fist, he hit the dashboard to smithereens.

He continued on foot towards in the road. After a hundred and fifty yards, he reached the first houses of the town. He passed an empty shop that had a flowerpot in its window. Casually, he glanced in the glass mirror. His gaze met a stranger. Is that me? Have I become another? Who or what has taken possession of me? His image in the glass showed an unshaven and emaciated man he hardly recognized. Mirror images have trouble with the truth, he considered. Shrugging, he continued on his way. There was little human traffic at this fairly early hour. "Even though I am not in a position to control the situation, I have the disadvantage in looking like a bum. A facelift is a prerequisite to fall out of tune. I lack money, and a reasonably educated person would say I'm a tramp. Human dignity is largely based on an inconspicuous appearance. They way you're dressed attracts attention at this time, but not as long as I don't fall out of place. Everyone who reads the papers will have the same bad taste as was his consideration when on the bike passed in an almost same outfit he wore."

After some time, Kosnic reached the town that had busier traffic. When he saw a police officer approaching him, he retraced his steps and went to a side street. With a detour, he finally reached the center. He saw a shopping center and a large department store. He waited patiently for a gallery to open before walking in. Through a side entrance, he went inside the warehouse. He kept a close surveillance as the passersby on the several stands. At a propitious moment, he managed to obtain a razor, blades, and a piece of shaving soap. He then went one floor up. He stripped himself of all his articles including the shredded cardboard and he threw the scraps into the toilet bowl and flushed them. Later, at the exit, the package won't alarm. He passed through and left the toilet. The ladies came out to the same output. There was also the seat of the retired teacher. In one of the toilets, they quarreled with a customer due to a dirty toilet bowl. And, almost noiselessly, Kosnic took the saucer that had a little money. "I can do that," he considered afterwards, when he was in the now crowded department store on his way to the exit. "If I ever get to live, I will repay her. "The weapon that's most dangerous here right now is your conscience. If I stay moral, I won't be able to protect myself," he said in a practical way. "Being yourself means being killed yourself," that was not a comment Ibsen would water. "How long has it been since I took some time to read something that amuses me?" he sighed. Maybe in the future, somewhere out there.

Half an hour later, in the hall of the station, he dodged two cops. They were equipped with a walkie-talkie and a revolver. Kosnic threw a dime in the machine of the toilet door. Quietly, he washed and he shaved himself. He wiped off the soap using toilet paper. "So Harry, you look back quite acceptable," he muttered. "Though a barber would not be luxurious and..." He was again overwhelmed by his reflection. "I nevertheless differ from what I look in the past," he noted. "Yeah, you can call it comfortable. It's the discrepancy between fact and self-esteem," he concluded. "You're older, leaner, and harder," his brows furrowed deep. "That's not surprising at all."

Suddenly, he noticed that the rats had the habit of starving them and it nearly devoured him. The body is boss on all fronts. At the factory, when his stomach scolded him, he had to fight his brain in taking a lump of sugar from the waste box. All munks had to resist the temptation. The only time you can have one is in the toilet but you have to be quick before a guard can catch you. If you were caught, they rigged you off with their batons and afterwards, you had to go without dinner. The cellmates would then offer a part of their meager meal to the victim.

Spying around attentively, Kosnic left the station.

In a busy supermarket, he stopped to buy a bar of chocolate and a piece of cheese. "Good for energy. I hope they'll get me through," he thought. He spent the rest of his cash on a carton of milk and half a loaf of bread.

"Would Emilie help me?" Since the day he was arrested at the factory, he rarely found time to think of Emilie. The image that he carried about her had become flattened and incomplete. "You feel lost and find yourself back in the quicksand of the past," he thought. "You think you've absorbed everything. The truth filtered through your memories and to the reality of the moment and reveals no more than lies. On the whole, reality is the name for a rather one-sided view. Just like vision," he corrected himself. How is Emilie faring at this time? Kosnic marveled at his indifference and lack of interest and shook his head. In a park, he sat on a bench. In such a position, he was able to feel at any side should that be necessary. Kosnic remained attentive to the environment. He ate his frugal meal of dry bread crumbs with cheese, a piece of chocolate, and drank the milk. "This is better than what I've eaten in the last period," he sighed. What remained of the bread and the cheese, he stuffed in his pockets. "Take a break, relax," he thought optimistically. However, even an optimist can end up in his coffin. Anyway, Emilie kept his mind occupied. Would it be safe to visit her? It seems better to set it aside for a while. He won't be surprised if they kept an eye on his house.

From the early years of their relationship, a trivial incident came to mind. It now seemed so far away and unreal, as if it were a snapshot of happiness. It was more than a brief rest in the unrest, he considered. Boredom still had not gnawed in their relationship. It was a time when he was lighter than air and he could fly as free as a bird and enjoy his youth. Happiness was based on the situation, not an idea. Oh, it was all bullshit! The recent years with Emilie have been eroded by ragged love and the trivialities of marriage, especially when there no more superficial spiritual contacts exist between partners. Their relationship was, for the most part, based on sex. And back then it seemed like a good idea to get married based on that, to make it last for as long as they can. A woman pours her heat in the hell of existence in the garbage heap of everydayness, if you want to call it that. A forgotten smile crept across Kosnic's face. In the recent months, he had almost forgotten how to laugh and he also forgot how to cry.

He'd need to find shelter for that day, he noted. The place must be flawless. Where can he find that? Security is like life. It dreams of death. Death remains your most loyal companion. Where can he find a quiet place to spend the night in this chilling world? Where do other hobos go? Do they just hustle off? Maybe an old neighborhood can offer some perspective like a staircase, an abandoned warehouse, or a ruin. There will be less police there, he suspected. The police, aware of their own safety, preferably choose the main roads. Of course, not all local police officers were equipped with a chipklikker. It was a shaky presumption. What he did not address yesterday can present itself today. At about midnight, he still hasn't found a place to stay. However, his luck wasn't in an unsympathetic mood. In the old south of the city where decay dominated, where the shadow of poverty was cast, the rent was low. Kosnic managed to find shelter there. Wrapped in the cloak of the night, he was systematically shunned by the community police officers.

In one of those streets, hidden from view by a moving truck along the sidewalk, there was an unpainted shop. The space behind the window functioned as a warehouse and office. It was a well-known place that went by the name "Cheaper than Cheap." Perhaps the owner was cheap, Kosnic wondered in a quirky mood. In the nearly empty shop were eight racks of women's clothing. Behind the railing of the staircase was a visible path that led to the basement. A wide staircase of six or eight steps led to the entrance of a higher space that had open sliding doors. He saw the contours of a small office that had two desks and a filing cabinet. On the street side of the property under the shop window, there was a basement window without glass. It was locked from the inside with a hardboard. Kosnic pushed against it with a rowdy shoe. The bow gave way a little and he gave a little more pressure. It proved to be a shot, which was put fixed with a pair of nails. The shot snapped back and fell to the basement floor with a lot of noise. Kosnic was startled. He knew he could've alarmed some neighbors or a few curious passers-by. He waited a few minutes. "In any case, I'm going to see if I can find shelter for the night," he decided. The incident triggered no response. All the windows of the houses remained dark. Apparently, no one paid attention to unfamiliar sounds. "You never interfere with anyone has he cooks fat," as was the motto of the neighborhood. Kosnic went back to the shop and explored the area. He noted where the cellar window was and decided to work on it. The dry basement floor confirmed his suspicion. He waited a few moments until his eyes became accustomed to the darkness. He groped along the walls and banged on the boxes. He saw blank stacks and racks of clothes. He found a light switch next to the door of the staircase that led to the shop. His hand hesitated on the switch. He dared not turn on the light. He fumbled back to the window. He knew how to easily access the switch. He turned on the light, a single bulb, and assessed the situation. He knew that despite the crack at the closed door at the bottom of the stairs, no light would leak out on the streets. This seemed to be an appropriate shelter for the night as long as no one was with him. You never knew who was walking along the street. He leveled a few blank stacks. He took some robes off a rack and put them on the cardboard. He turned off the light and lay down on his makeshift bed and covered himself with a few coats. "I must not grumble," he sighed, relaxed. "Maybe I can spend a few nights here until I find something better. Coincidence is the leader in this kind of life. I'll have to get used to it. A minimum existence is enough. The office upstairs probably has a small greenhouse with some money. That's the price I have to give for this accommodation. Once I plunder that cash, the company will know that there was a break in and the window will be restored. By that time, I'll have to say farewell to this place!" He felt exhausted but now he could finally relax. The previous night, he failed falling asleep. Now, he could surrender to sleep!

The next morning at about half past seven, Kosnic rose from his sleep. He could hear the sounds of the street. A reluctant car tried to start up. The chill had awakened him. With some difficulty, he could remember where he was. Shuddering, he lit the light. He washed his face a little at a fountain. A bathrobe served as a towel. Suddenly, he became aware of his situation and he felt free. To avoid leaving traces, he put back the things in their original place. In a cluttered closet with cleaning articles, he found a mop. He dried up the fountain. Nobody could ever guess that a vagrant had spent the night here. In one of the large boxes, he sought a pair of jeans that suited him. Before returning to the outside world, he turned out the light and listened if anyone was on the sidewalk. He shot slightly to the side and peered through a crack in the dimly lit street in both directions. Outside, dawn was approaching. His side was free. On the other side, he could see some parked cars. As long as nobody crossed, he could crawl unseen from the basement. Once outside, he pulled the shot gently back into place. It would be his shelter for tonight, too.

The firm's owner, after some time, harbored the suspicion that someone was staying overnight in the basement. In the basement was a coat used by two staff members who worked on top of the office. One of these employees, as he typed the previous day had her tin with a slice of bread for the birds, forgotten. That bread was gone the next morning. It could not have been rats, unless rats could open drums. The mop has been used but it was not put back in its place. Yet, none of the office ladies have used a mop. The owner had no tangible evidence. The room was not cluttered. In the past, he had to repair the window a few times. A few months later, it was smashed again and some goods were missing. If a tramp was using the basement as a place to sleep, then others would come overnight and steal the goods, he considered. He pondered the matter over and decided to tolerate it for the time being.

In the market stall, Kosnic bought some tools such as pliers, a screwdriver, and some keys. After a prolonged fumbling up to the late evening, he learned how machines could open for food and if necessary, to get some money. To avoid starting a manhunt, he spread these activities across different neighborhoods. He bought two or three articles in supermarkets. Fearful of the monitors who were placed at various points to check the customers, he stole the rest of the food he needed. On one of those days, a large daily market which was always something to find him, he ran behind a row of stalls along the houses. Two officers lounged in the middle between the stalls. Kosnic kept a close eye on them. He suddenly saw Emilie, shopping. The blind chance fixated both his eyes. He growled. In reality, he knew that it means, to be understood, to remain in the tiny blankly.

He followed Emilie for a short distance. He was waiting for a suitable moment to approach her. She was startled and pale when she saw her husband suddenly appear beside her. "I look like I'm the devil himself," Kosnic thought. Nervously, she pulled her left shoulder forward.

"Are you really Harry? You're alive?"

"As I am. I died a thousand deaths and am resurrected again. Life is fragile, but I can't get enough of it yet."

His remark passed failed to elicit a response. For that moment, he forgot that he has a sense of humor.

"You've changed. I was shocked. I thought you've forsaken me," she recoiled in uncertainty. "Walk on," he said compellingly. He feared that she was being shadowed. He noticed that she felt uncomfortable. He walked a lot with her. Now and then, along the stalls, he saw a passer-by who had happened to be going in the same direction as them. She had changed, he noted. She has become fuller. Had she fared better without him? She pulled her shoulder back.

"You let me down," she repeated disapprovingly.

"What could I do about it? I was arrested at my job."

"And how was I supposed to make a living? You know I can't cope alone."

What could this mean? Were all this honesty, vulnerability, stupidity, and aggressive language posed to shock him? No, there was a certain degree of intelligence necessary. Kosnic searched for his words. Had he forgotten how to start an everyday conversation after all the fragmentary whispers in the cell and in the factory?

"No trouble with the police?" he inquired, to make follow through with the conversation.

"The police came by twice and asked me if I knew where you were. A patrolling agent comes in the house once in a while to drink coffee. Have you done something wrong?"

Kosnic shook his head and sighed.

"Not at all." It seemed wise to vent his story, but there was no time. Additionally, he felt responsible for her safety.

"Nothing at all? How can that be? You won't be free..." she broke in the middle of the sentence. "Where are you living?"

It seemed unwise to share his temporary residence with her.

"I wander the streets. I am a refugee," In the corner of his eye, he saw the two cops from the market lounge approaching. Would it be safe to rely on Emilie? He nodded at her and wanted to retrace his steps.

"How do you live?" she asked.

"In thievery," he growled and was picked up by the crowd that moved forward in the opposite direction.

He shot between two stalls through to the back where he had some free walking space. He kept on watching if he was being followed or not. When he had the impression that the coast was clear, he returned. His eyes searched the area where he had spotted Emilie. She had gone. Unsatisfied, he shook his head. He had so much to say to her. Emilie's words, usually behind upwellings aanholden, could not be controlled. It made him confused. In retrospect, nothing was enlightening about it. Naturally, he had a fairly broad view of things. Emilie can't conduct herself to a meaningful conversation, he knew from experience. As a rule, he projected his importance and interest. Never before was it so clear in his mind. He shook his head and thought of their mutual "love," or what was left of it. He missed the sobriety, but he was able to gain insight into the situation. Did he lack common sense? Even common sense would know that hiding in the attic is nonsense! Nonsense reigns supremely. There are not many people who can sober up and use their mental faculties abstractly. However, it cherishes views and wants a say. Emilie lives in the deflated balloon of airspace. In practical terms, she could occasionally show some interest for the world. That turns out to be pretty primitive construction. Ergo, reality remains dependent on the general madness of individuals. Overall, we can only sniff a little bit of reality and truth. "What I could have told her? That I loved her? She knew that already. The question is, do I love her seriously? Was there such a thing as undying love? Love is like a biochemical glitch on the shady side of truth and knowledge. And truth is a striptease of facts."

It was not easy for Kosnic that day. The evening was drizzly. The chilly drizzle made the greasy pavement shine in the lachrymose light of the street lamps. Even the sky languished. On the way to his hideout, he turned to a corner that had a canal. He nearly collided with two agents. One of them wore a chipklikker, which immediately started tapping and blinking. They walked into the middle of the street, eight meters from Kosnic. He turned quickly and ran back along the old houses of the canal. The cops, busy talking at the shop, stared at each other blankly for a moment and went headlong into the chase.

"Stop or I'll shoot!"

They both fired single shots. The echo ran along the shuddering canal houses. Kosnic was just able to turn into another lane. Life is notorious for its uninhabitable, he considered panting. I really need to do something about my condition."

He went to a brothel. A customer was just leaving. The forced Venus from the Red Palace appeared in the doorway and Kosnic saw her approaching. Her exuberant cleavage and enthusiastic blared out, which legitimized the suspicion that she was on sale for another crusader.

"Hello darling," she said to Kosnic "Come inside."

"No time," he gasped, "police." He was about to run past.

"Come quickly." They grabbed him by the shoulder and he staggered inside. She glanced at the street corner, but no one appeared. "At the back, flat on the couch."

Kosnic rushed into the house and did what he was told. The couch was still lukewarm from her previous job. As usual, they left the door ajar. She came behind him and climbed on top of him. She unzipped his fly and ran expertly over the sluggish torch within. Just as according to her vocation, he immediately felt the flashes of flames in his groin.

"It is hot. We do so but, save a Jassie. "

Anonymous addressed disappeared stroking his pole somewhere in its subway. The emotion of my faithful follower affords a different kind of sex that I would allow him. The owner is considered helpless. Apparently, he likes strange beliefs. Maybe more so. His guardian angel unhooked her Ballennet and she buried her quivering flaunts in his face. Meanwhile, she heaved her body like a lifeboat in rough seas. A Greek Orthodox cross dangled between her packed breasts, and they unmistakably begged for support. But, nevertheless, was not enough to lift the result above the level of a shop daughter in double meaning. With frequent use, this priestess of social love had worn to a cliché. But still!

"Come, come to mother Mary, boy. I understand. But fuck me! We only live once and this is too much!"

The agents had missed their prey as they turned the corner of the street. Their eyes wandered through the alley.

"Mary! Mary!" There yelled at the door.

"There they are, those riffraff. They've lost you, hunk."

She raised her head.

"What do you want?" she shouted toward the door.

"Have you seen a guy running somewhere here?"

"My ass. I've spent the past half an hour pumping my tail off the clock." She said as she hugged Kosnic.

Grinning, the cops left and began searching for their target elsewhere.

Kosnic let his imagination run wild. Mary was no Emilie at all!

"Won't you come for me a few times?" she went professional. "It gives me a huge boost to know I've made that rig happy more than once." She sighed, relaxing. "Stay Effies so Legge."

"I can't pay you."

"Thunders nothing comes later. Exactly Bartje me, I thought you did an Renne. Choose tight, I want your story baby."

Kosnic began to perspire under this voluptuous lady. Moments, later she rose slowly to her feet.

"Not included by walking. I'll immediately close the tent. Genog goodwill themed fenavunt. You've got a home?"

"I have no home."

She looked at him. Her hard features softened as she girded her hammock. From the divan, Kosnic followed this scene. She was the type of woman you would assume was created out of ruin. But still, amidst her care for the baby was a shell of modesty. He glanced at his lust bat. After the timid attempt to look jaunty, it was now a dangling thing; a beaten beast of burden. Sex and good taste are avid antipodes. To dry his little business and fashion, she gave him a service. He wiped his listless lubber off and locked him in his pants. I he was part of the harvest for the day. He put on his newly ironed jeans and T-shirt on.

"You are welcome to an hour's blaave. I want to make and eat a glaasie. You may have aagelek blaave her lie also axis that you want, young." She stroked him his hair lovingly.

"And at my age," he smonzelde.

"Me Bartje thought to manifest a splash adorn with a brown line pressure. Well, he's been spending years abroad in jail. Two years later, I received a smuggled letter. But first, we do a hektortje, sweetie." She walked forward, put out the light in the window where they had fucked before, and closed the door.

Kosnic found another refuge. It was in an old school that used to be a workspace for artists years ago. The modest tools that he had proved useful in many services. He managed to open the large lock at the front door. It was easier than he had expected. Half the space in the building was unused. The bare walls were littered with bad paintings. Kosnic noted that every morning at eight o'clock, a concierge appeared who turned on the heater and performed some work. Before that that time, he must get out. In the evening between six and eight, two workers kept the place clean for the next day. After which, he could finally go inside. It was a less drafty shelter than the basement shelter. Moreover, it was less cold.

Kosnic pondered regularly at the chip in his shoulder. How could he get rid of the thing!? "As long as I walk around with these torpedoes, I am stigmatized. I can't live like this; like a hunted wild animal. They can shoot me anytime. By chance, I can walk into a trap. I should have stayed with the Doerningroep," he thought for the umpteenth time. They might have had a solution to get rid you of the chip. Can respect ever be found for a refugee? Can one live a life without fear? "Maybe I can reconnect with Emilie? Whatever am I going to do with Emilie?" She was the last straw. He'd have to wait some more before they can be together again. But would it be sufficient? Can they still be partners despite the broken illusions? Why Emilie? As long as the possibility exists for him to distance himself from the latter, if necessary, it will remain an advantage. Or was there another way? He owed himself the mystery. He was back on square one. The past is mainly determined by the things you did or wanted to do, things that have remained undone, and things that could have been done. "Emilie! You must have something to live for, Harry! The road to Emilie requires an income and a job. Where can I work when I have this chip in my arm?" The primary problem remains. He now had to find a reliable doctor who won't rat him out. But revealing himself is by itself too risky. A chipklikker which can disable the reaction isn't particularly ideal but it would suffice.

Ten days later in the early evening, the stars nestled hesitantly on the hazy veil of night. An unforeseen opportunity occurred to him. Kosnic sat in a park behind the bushes on a stone ledge. He was eating a dry slice of bread with some cheese on it. With his back, he leaned against a concrete fence. It was a fairly quiet time. Outside, aside from the leaving office clerk or salesperson, nobody was in the park. At about six meters away, a regular police officer passed by. He was decorated with the usual equipment and he carried a worn briefcase under his arm. Apparently, he was on his way home. Kosnic saw from a distance that the chipklikker he was carrying on his belt was inoperative. Suddenly, the officer lost his stride. He slipped to a bulky oak left of the lane, across the bushes where Kosnic was hiding behind. He took off his cap and peered around the tree. A man behind the high bushes stood by a sloping hill that led to a small pond. Nearby, two young people were having sex. Kosnic followed the scene with the agent and understood what it was about. He had come to see the couple. In a flash, a plan sparked in his mind. He slid his last crust of bread naturally back in the paper and he put it in his pocket. The other hand surrounded the rock in his pocket. "Let us steal our power in the night," he recalled. I can do that, he hesitated. Ethics can't be factor now, Harry knew. "Ethics is discussed in a favorable environment," he soothed his conscience. If he was ever discovered, then he'd only have a minute to live. His moral considerations were crippling. This was an opportunity that he should not run from. One well-aimed blow to the head, and the guard would be knocked out for some time. Kosnic rose slowly to his feet and hesitated. He moved on forward, soothing his conscience. Faust chimed in, or was it the devil? His heart beat faster. He was nervous. And if he fails, then what? So what! He who goes through life without a struggle isn't worth it. "Denying fear is useless, Harry". With a pounding heart, he crept to the voyeur. Doesn't he have something better to do than to spy on the fucking couple? Anyway, at that moment, Harry Kosnic struck the agent in his head just as the agent stretched his neck and leaned forward. It was a fatal blow. The sleeve missed the hard skull, but his vertebra was shattered. Without even uttering a sigh, the agent fell. A cold wind blew and Kosnic felt that it was good. In the distance in the horizon, he heard someone singing: "Nobody knows the trouble I've seen..."

God's ways are inscrutable. Still. People choose for themselves. He washed his hands in the pond of innocence where a used condom bobbed around. Kosnic's hands seemed to have been shocked by the result. At first glance, he seemed to have died of horror. Those two had not noticed it were lost in the real delight of knowing each other. Or below. Kosnic frantically looked around. There was no one around. Nervously, he dragged the victim behind the bushes. Kosnic took his chipklikker, his belt and his revolver. Whoever this dead person was no longer proved useful. Kosnic patted some dust off his jacket. He pulled of the guard's tunic that was too wide for him. He moved the tools from his old jacket to the pockets of the new outfit. He didn't forget to empty the pockets of his new jacket. He was allowed to keep his snotlap as a palliative. At the beginning of the lane, Kosnic heard someone approaching. Suddenly, he realized the bag and cap of the victim was left behind the tree. For a moment, he panicked. With difficulty, he managed to control himself. He indifferently wriggled himself on his fly as if he were Watergeus that just spoke the spell of the wild. The pseudo-agent walked to the tree and snatched the police hat and bag off the ground. He casually nodded at the passerby. Kosnic cast a furtive glance at the lovers in the pond. The Feast of Eros was over and they arranged their clothing. Kosnic returned to the dead policeman and waited impatiently behind the bushes until he saw the couple leave. Darkness was falling fast. When the scattered light of a lantern and the twilight of the lighted windows were behind the fence, he thought he discerned dark spots on policeman's dead face. He bent down to see better. It proved to be a termite. Before covering the corpse with his old jacket, he checked again if all pockets were stripped of their contents. His nervous hands trembled. In conclusion, he dragged the body to a shallow pit just down the garden wall and covered it with a layer of decaying leaves. For a few moments, he looked down on this makeshift grave as if to reflect on his actions; as if he wanted to apologize to the dead and wished him peace. Death had stunned him, like life had.

"I actually did not desire this," Kosnic sighed. It sounded like an apology; a thin excuse. He turned away. He was also a victim of the regime. In any case, the dead agent won't need to polish his brass buttons. The worms and ants will take care of him.

Kosnic threw the murder weapon in the pond and washed his hands. He found a second condom, as if God had seen the wiggles of joy that went up and down as in his last operational phase.

The tunic was too broad for Kosnic, as well as the belt. He dropped the cap down to his ears. Everything was correct. With the bag under one arm, he walked through the deserted avenues where he was shortly before. Across the park just outside the halo of a lantern, he checked how the chip could be neutralized by the chipklikker. In the past, his cellmates had informed each other in whispers how it would work. He tried it out. Indeed, the clicker did not react to the chip in his shoulder. A special apparatus should be only coming to activate the chip again. He put the clicker in the neutral position and the lock in a pocket. He did not risk keeping the thing within reach. He buckled the belt to fit him. In a trash, he found a newspaper.

He tore it up and put in the tube of the cap. "Voila," he thought. "Now the cap fits me just right."

He wanted to continue his way when suddenly he was overcome by the realization that he has just killed his fellow man. He gasped at the thought which overwhelmed him. "Now I'm one of them," he panted. Perplexed, he stopped when he realized that. "I have committed murder for my own freedom! Is freedom worth killing another man? My freedom is tainted and violated!"

Harry Kosnic's mind wandered back to the uprising in the factory. There were other men murdered for the sake of freedom. So what could he do? Allow himself to be enslaved? That was not on the agenda. The death of a cop was not intentional, he tried to justify himself. "I had, in advance, should have realize that it could go wrong. There is no excuse for doing this. The system not only sets the monster loose in oneself, it does way worse than that," he considered bitterly. "In every human being dwells a potential killer. Never let the monster within you arise or steal the glimmer of light in your mind." Now what? Panting with emotion, he sank down on a bench and stared at the dark void within him.

Kosnic remained there until he managed to get himself back under control. The last glimmer of starlight in the sky has already been engulfed by clouds. He stood up and jadedly walked towards the old school building on the canal. He wanted to go to sleep early to try to forget his troubles. The knowledge that the chip was off offered little consolation. His gaze turned to the canal. The cleaning ladies were already gone. A few minutes later, he walked through the dark corridors. He had a flashlight with him, but he blindly found his way in the building. A few months ago, an artist left a rickety leather couch in the first floor. The upholstery was battered, that much is true. But it was good enough for Kosnic. He now wanted to get some rest after this eventful day. "My safety is guaranteed. This is the opportunity to flee with Emilie abroad and build a new life.

On the other hand, wouldn't it be wise if I benefit in my current bachelorhood. I need to first reconcile with my internal killer. The question is, if I can, would I succeed? I don't want to be reduced to a state of penance. That would be ridiculous. But still! What else could I do? How can I recover from this debt? Why don't I just shoot myself? Self-preservation transcends destructiveness. The easiest way proves the most difficult. The choices are important. It's a step that I can't take." He shook his head. "Harry Kosnic, you've caught yourself in the chokepoints of your life. You lack the courage to puke it out. Whatever happens makes little difference. The deed has been done manifest whether or not you live. But for as long as you live, the debt will continue to stare at you from the background."

"Clichés, mere clichés," he sighed wearily. I have to control myself so I don't get overwhelmed by my internal violence. It is difficult to control the chaos of your chaos. Whatever luck befalls you, it will never serve as an excuse to remind you to pull up your life. If you ever want to get off, it will be a pointless suicide."

"I'll turn to my own navel," he decided. "It makes me crazy! Existence is meaningless!" In his pocket, he felt a small thickness of the remaining bread crust and brought it out. To dispel the bad taste in his mouth, he bit a piece off and chewed at it. It was bland, but for a moment it was able to take his mind off heavier things. His gaze fell on the bag. He examined its contents: a pair of white gloves, keys, a set of handcuffs, a notepad, a lunch box held together by a rubber band, and a small round flashlight. He emptied the pockets of his jacket with the aid of a flashlight. He found a police whistle and some spectacles. In another pocket, he found a pen and an old book. There was some paper money, a credit card, and a driver's license. The man's name was Mihajlo Vasko Friedmann. In the last box, he found a picture of a woman and two small children. Kosnic ran to the bathroom, pulled off the tunic that hung on the window, and turned on the light. He sat on the lid of the toilet seat and studied the photo and the license. "Why would a cheerful man, married to a kind woman, father of two children, unscrupulously serve this order? Because they needed food? Was there no other way to make a living? How is it possible that an ordinary, seemingly decent citizen such as Friedmann has commissioned himself to a rigid regime? What am I? I'm just the murderer of this man! That remains to be seen. I'm a desperado. I pushed myself to be extremely desperate. My circumstances were as such. What is the role of the police in general? Maintaining authority and public order, protecting citizens against crime? But their purpose does not matter. Such a situation is invariably at the expense of the citizen. This means that they can contradict each other under certain circumstances. Anyway, at a decisive moment, you have to say "No." For the so-called "authorities," that equally applies. The question is, can they intervene in a conditional crisis on an individual choice? Although, if Friedmann had caught me then, should I take that into account?" He sighed. "We are, in this case, not morally obliged by the words "if." I wouldn't ever know, so I should suspend my judgment. Man appears to be capable of anything. We can't understand ourselves but we somehow get involved with a lot of suffering. For the future, surviving remains the same. Do the police ever go against their training and consciences? And the older agents; were they required to sign a declaration of loyalty accompanied by a description of the consequences? Would I have signed such a statement? That's not the problem. Other factors play a major role." Kosnic felt bitter. He was a murderer. For the rest of his life, he must carry the burden with him. "We were born for death. Death is an everyday thing but not as long as you live. And for myself, I'm a manmade monster. Each person is responsible for his choices as well as for his actions. Suppose it was a retaliation for some bestial treatment? Then it would be called revenge. Revenge is for those who want to cherish the past. Was it coincidence? Coincidence is the marriage between heaven and hell, between man and monster." Unwittingly, a tear dripped on his hands. Murderous hands. The hands that kept sweating. "I can always invent another alibi. Morality does not determine the situation. The situation determines morality and that is madness. The animal becomes human. It is disastrous to be a human fiend. We should pay attention to the capacity of our brutality and be aware of what it does to us."

"This is an anti-human system and I am one of them. I am a gangster. And a gangster can only go so far. But what do I mean? If Friedmann had a bad conscience, he wouldn't have helped me. What could he have done if he had discovered me? He now enjoys the benefit of his death. He is exempted from life, of violence, of murder, and fear of death. How could a dead man be familiar with this miserable world? His celebration should be without end and without anyone whatsoever." His thoughts and feelings moved in a circle.

"I want to live, but not under these circumstances. Or is it? Is this a way of life? The tragedy of life is a rubbish heap."

Kosnic tried to think of his victims. Friedmann's wife and children were also victims. "I now possess sufficient resources to live at the expense of agent Friedmann. When I am on the border and find work, I will pay back everything. I can't give Friedmann back. That would be impossible. Tomorrow, I will ask Emilie what she wants. I don't deserve better. Emilie can do what she wants."

Continued to be violated by his deed, Kosnic wandered around the city the next. He rejected the idea to go back to the park and to investigate whether he had left traces. He knows that any perpetrator who returns to the crime scene is a waiting disaster. But what about his footprints? He didn't think of that, and he dismayed. What if there were sniffer dogs around? He must strictly avoid the park and buy new shoes.

With the money he obtained from Friedmann, he bought a pair of shoes at a stall at the market. He then threw his old shoes in a bin. That afternoon, he entered a cafe and ordered the daily special. How long has it been since he's eaten anything reasonable? The past seemed to be a bygone era now. Will there ever come a time when he'll repay all those he was indebted with?

Two days later, Kosnic was able to find his way to his former home. When crossing the busy station, he unexpectedly stumbled upon a demonstration. He wanted to avoid the crowds but suddenly, policemen suddenly appeared on all sides. The cops, helmeted and equipped with shields, rushed to the infidel mass. The crowd seemed violent. A police crowd is murderous. Kosnic tried to escape. But out of nowhere, suddenly, a sergeant in uniform came from behind. He grabbed Kosnic by the shoulder.

"Officer second class, your colleagues need you and you're not coming to the rescue?"

"I'm out of service," Kosnic stammered.

"You can forget that for a moment," snarled the other, "Come follow me."

Kosnic had no choice but to obey or else he would arouse suspicion.

"With the flat cap."

Flat cap? What does that mean? The chief had pulled his langelat and threw himself into the fray. Kosnic grabbed his rubber truncheon. The strap slipped naturally to his wrist. He let the stream of events float randomly, aware that he was hitting whoever he could hit. The crowd fled to the other side of the square. They were met by a second group of crusaders.

"You don't touch them! You're not a district nurse, I hope," shouted the sergeant. Kosnic saw the ecstasy in the eyes of the other who indulged in this one-sided battle. "Here they come again."

A group of protesters drove to their direction. Among them, an old man hobbled by. He clearly didn't know what to do. He ended up in the mass of demonstrators and was searching desperately for a way out. Kosnic thought he recognized something in him. The sergeant gave the man a push in his direction. The old man lost his balance and as a result, Kosnic swung his langelat and hit the old man fully in the head. It definitely was not his intention. The victim screamed and fell unconscious. Kosnic felt the tears came out of his eyes. The price he was paying for freedom seemed to have no end!

"Fine," shouted the chief beside him, "We'll get them, that scoundrel. Your eyes are wet."

"Sweat," growled Kosnic curtly.

"Here they come again," exulted the other in ecstasy.

From several sides, shots sounded. A number of civilians, including a terrified mother, tried to flee between the police. She was anxiously carrying a crying child on one hand and a sign in the other. The group ran towards a shop where it hoped to be safe. The chief jumped upon to choke them off and raised his arm with the bat. Impulsively, Kosnic let the langelat go and pulled the revolver. Two bullets found their way. Before he could strike the sergeant, he was hit in his back. Tense, he nodded his knees and slumped forward like a praying Muslim.

Most citizens now had to find a safe haven. There was a single shot from a side street. The station was swept by the police hurdle. Some protesters were handcuffed and thrown into riots cars. Ambulances wailed as they went back and forth picking up the dead and wounded. Kosnic did not wait for this. After his performance, he hastily removed himself from the battlefield. Through an entrance to a platform and a transition at the end, he slipped into an adjacent street rail. Frantically, he clutched the bag under his left arm as if it was his greatest treasure. With his mind at the old man, he threw the bag in the gutter. Five paces onwards, he realized that there were in shaving and other paraphernalia. He went back, bent down, and took the bag under his arm.

"Cowboy with his cauliflower, a turd spot. I hope he does not die. Even power makes God a devil." The image of the sergeant who collapsed was embedded in his retina. "It was exactly what he deserves," he thought bitterly. He paused, as if struck by lightning. Something was wrong. He felt another gap in his morality! "You walked over to the side of the opponents, Harry Kosnic, and was held hostage by your emotions. Such an institution gives your opponents equal rights to eliminate you as well! Albeit on different grounds, but that is irrelevant. It's about morality. What can you bring to contradict that, Harry Kosnic?" Entangled in such considerations, he continued on his way. "You should also protect yourself," he realized. "Think on! There are more people than monsters and victims. Revenge is disastrous. Try to find a way however difficult it may be."

Kosnic aimlessly wandered through the city. His thoughts were fixed on that one-sided battle. The image of the bleeding old man would not budge from his retina. His cry beat on his conscience. Desperately, he shook his head. Will this ever end? Despair and an impotent aggression teased his mind. Groaning of impotence, he wandered through the city. This was not the most appropriate time to see Emilie. If she ever finds anything out, she would loathe me as I loathe myself.

For the rest of the day, Kosnic philosophized anything that crossed his mind. "What a world is this that's too sad to live in. Life isn't possible without violence. Scruples are useless if violence arises. To be a part of if it to be equally infected and stigmatized. The dead remain anonymous. Tomorrow, when I speak with Emilie, I'll first buy a dark gray jacket, the sort everyone wears in the market, and a cap. I dressed me evening in the school. That police gang I dump into the canal, except chipklikker and revolver. If they ever arrest me, I will sell my life's duration. Once a murderer, always a murderer." A moment later he shook his head again in his aggression. "Violence is contagious. My biggest enemy is myself," he murmured.

Two days later, Kosnic believed that he was now fit to see Emilie. He sauntered into the afternoon to his former address, rang the doorbell, and waited. Emilie opened the door. She had a tear-stained face and moist eyes. "Blue as in jelly," the thought shot through him.

"Emilie, we have nothing to fear anymore. I am one of them," he rattled in monotone as if he had memorized the text. She took him in silence. Was she marveled at his unusual outfit? Her skirt was protruding. Her belly bulged ostentatiously forward. Was she pregnant!? His forehead wrinkled. Wasn't the thought of having children adverse to them? She had never wanted to surrender to that odious and despised idea of motherhood. And now, he noted, Emilie was maternal. Who could well be the drummer? When was the last time they had slept together? He could no longer recall. Has it been that long since he got arrested? Since he escaped? It takes nine months to bear a child to the world. A split second helped him. What was the meaning of procreation if it existed in ignorance and violence? Reproduction is countered by propagation. In her lap she holds a child for the future, but there will be no future.

"It's you," Emilie was uncontrollably sobbing. He saw her face contorting. A sea of misery was about to burst from her eyelids.

"In a demonstration..." her body shook uncontrollably, "He had nothing to do with it... My poppa was beaten on his head. He... he is dying."

Kosnic's heart winced. The tips of his fingers tingled. Now, it was clear to him why the face he saw was so familiar. He, as infidel dog, who had been there for years been less welcome. Emilie had maintained contacts. A few years, she wished she could have a birthday with her large family. Kosnic fell back on what happened two days ago. It seemed that all blood flow stopped going to his head. Behind Emilie loomed an unfamiliar man who wore jeans and a dark blue jacket with brass buttons. He had almost the same stature as Harry Kosnic. The man put his arm around Emilie and pressed her against him.

"You okay, lovey?"

"Thank you, Bartje," she sobbed. Her face turned to his shoulder, seeking solace. It was Bartje!

"Is there anything going on, colleague?" He turned to Kosnic.

Harry Kosnic looked at him, bewildered. He was someone who looked suspiciously like him. He was almost his image, he could tell. Even the differences showed some similarities. "Is he... another me? Or am I..."

"No... It's nothing," he stammered blankly. "I just came to express my sorrow." For a moment, he stared sideways with his head bowed.

He realized the despair in his arms and legs. But his heart was missing. This person was something he must overcome. "But by myself? This is the end. We are ready for a new creation. Nature is forever. We are of secondary importance."

As if in a trance, Harry Kosnic nodded at his image. He then turned away and was unsure if he would ever find his way. He was lost in a labyrinth of thoughts and emotions.

The window of a tobacconist displayed the front page that morning with a big head: government cases. Because of that "legalized" Some of the ABP?

At the bottom left was short message:

"Under the influence of high pressure from the west, some sunny spells are expected..."

Could it still be a late spring?

* Helmuth Plessner. ** John Cowper Powys.

CPSIA information can be obtained at www.ICGtesting.com
Printed in the USA
BVOW03s1047060415

394875BV00001B/4/P

9 781681 224084